THE
BLING QUEEN

Also by Allison Gutknecht

Don't Wear Polka-Dot Underwear with White Pants
(And Other Lessons I've Learned)

A Cast Is the Perfect Accessory
(And Other Lessons I've Learned)

Never Wear Red Lipstick on Picture Day
(And Other Lessons I've Learned)

Pizza Is the Best Breakfast
(And Other Lessons I've Learned)

THE
BLING QUEEN

Allison Gutknecht

aladdin M!X

ALADDIN M!X
New York London Toronto Sydney New Delhi

m!x

ALADDIN M!X
Simon & Schuster Children's Publishing Division
1230 Avenue of the Americas, New York, New York 10020
First Aladdin M!X edition September 2016
Text copyright © 2016 by Simon & Schuster, Inc.
Cover illustration copyright © 2016 by Annoosha Syed
Also available in an Aladdin hardcover edition.
All rights reserved, including the right of reproduction in whole or in part in any form.
ALADDIN is a trademark of Simon & Schuster, Inc., and related logo is a registered trademark of Simon & Schuster, Inc. | ALADDIN M!X and related logo are registered trademarks of Simon & Schuster, Inc. | For information about special discounts for bulk purchases, please contact Simon & Schuster Special Sales at 1-866-506-1949 or business@simonandschuster.com. | The Simon & Schuster Speakers Bureau can bring authors to your live event. For more information or to book an event, contact the Simon & Schuster Speakers Bureau at 1-866-248-3049 or visit our website at www.simonspeakers.com.
Cover designed by Jessica Handelman
Interior designed by Steve Scott
The text of this book was set in Bodoni Egyptian Pro.
Manufactured in the United States of America 0816 OFF
10 9 8 7 6 5 4 3 2 1
Library of Congress Control Number 2015959858
ISBN 978-1-4814-5309-7 (hc)
ISBN 978-1-4814-5308-0 (pbk)
ISBN 978-1-4814-5310-3 (eBook)

For Sara Bender and Bridget Highet,
who prove that the only accessories
you need in middle school
are your best friends

THE
BLING QUEEN

Chapter 1

Let me tell you the problem with a glitter belt—it's the glitter.

I learned my lesson with glitter belts last year, but Deirdre, not so much. Which is why, one by one, piece by piece, I am picking teeny specks of glitter out of Deirdre's thick strands of red hair. Her hair is so long that its tips sway against the edge of her belt, capturing glitter like wisps of dandelion in a windstorm.

That's kind of poetic, actually—"wisps of dandelion in a windstorm." If I were writing in my language arts journal right now like I'm supposed to be doing, instead of systematically pulling glitter off Deirdre's head, I might jot that down.

"Ow!" Deirdre whisper-yells from her seat in front of me. "Do you have to pull so hard?"

"I think you meant to say 'thank you,'" I whisper back to her. "I warned you not to wear that belt again." She leans back in her seat and shakes her hair over my desk, two flakes of glitter depositing themselves on my notebook. I tap the back of her head with the tip of my green gel pen—my Thursday color, since it's my second-favorite— like a stick on a snare drum. *Tap tappity tap, tappity tap, tappity tap*—

WHOOSH. Deirdre whirls around in her seat, her glittery hair flying around her, undoubtedly spraying the rest of the room. She and I face off silently, the tiny crinkles at the edges of her eyes matching the ones on the sides of my lips. We call this "glirking"—a glaring smirk. When you're annoyed but also entertained, want to smack the other person but also want to laugh out loud, you glirk.

Deirdre and I glirk at each other quietly until she tries to swipe my pen out of my hand, and I am forced to throw my arm up into the air to escape her reach, acci- dentally tossing my pen onto the floor as I do. Deirdre covers her mouth with her hand, shoulders shaking as she tries not to laugh out loud, while I get up to retrieve the pen.

"Girls," Ms. Castleby calls from her desk, dragging out the word with a lilt in her voice, so that I can tell she's not actually angry with us.

I take my seat as Deirdre turns to face the front of the room, and then I look over to Bree's desk. She shakes her head, laughing with no sound.

"The belt," I mouth to her, pointing to Deirdre's waist. "I *told* her."

"I know," Bree mouths back just as the bell rings.

"That's all for today, people." Ms. Castleby walks to the front of the room as we gather our things. She barely looks much older than us, though she's been teaching at Twining Ridge Middle School since at least last year. I know because I remember seeing her in the hallways— or more specifically, I remember seeing her outfits. Ninety-nine percent of her ensemble will be normal, and then—bam!—there's always one piece that catches your eye. Today it's a scarf that she has tied around the front of her hair like a headband. The scarf is white with tiny yellow stars sprinkled across it, which match her hair perfectly.

I love everything about it.

"Remember, tomorrow I'm collecting your journals to read and to grade, so if all of your entries aren't complete, I suggest you finish them up tonight." The rest of the class lets out a collective moan, but I don't join them. I kind of like the journal. Ms. Castleby gives us a topic to write about each day, in case we're out of ideas, but she's also okay if we do our own thing. So all of my

3

entries are about clothes, or shoes, or jewelry, or bags, or hair accessories. I almost never write in my journal in class, like we're supposed to. Instead I do all of the work at home, so I can make each entry perfect.

This is the first time Ms. Castleby is collecting our journals for a grade. And even though I don't usually care about my grades as much as I should (or at least, as much as my parents think I should), I really hope she gives me a high mark. Not even because I want to prove my parents' "You need to focus more on school and less on fashion, Tess" decree wrong, but because this journal is actually fun for me.

But of course, if Ms. Castleby likes my journal as much as I do, well, that certainly wouldn't hurt, especially if it resulted in an A+. That way I could show it to my parents and say, "See? Writing about fashion isn't only *one way* to get good grades. It's the *best way* to get good grades!" This is an especially important point to prove to them right now, since in a few weeks, an antique-jewelry exhibition is coming to a museum near us, and Mom and Dad said we can't go unless I start becoming more "conscientious." That's their word of the year, it seems—"conscientious." And specifically how I am *not* conscientious.

"Also, I'll be assigning your business plan projects tomorrow," Ms. Castleby continues as our class begins to file out of her room. I wait for Deirdre to finish unty-ing (yes, untying) her sneakers before I trail her to the classroom door.

"Deirdre, aren't you going to trip like that?" Ms. Castleby asks.

"I tuck the laces into the sides of my unitard—see?" Deirdre explains. "The shoes are more comfortable that way." Deirdre pulls back the side of her sneaker, revealing the hooks of her stirrup pants hidden under-neath. I know she needs her unitard for gymnastics practice later, but it still seems silly for her to insist on wearing it under her clothes all day. I roll my eyes at Ms. Castleby behind Deirdre's back, and she smiles knowingly.

"Move it along, whackadoo," I say, nudging Deirdre toward the door. "Bree, are you coming?"

"Yeah, yeah," Bree answers, cradling her flute case in her arms like it's a newborn.

"You know, you could leave that in your locker," I point out. "It's not like you play the tuba and it won't fit." We all wave to Ms. Castleby as we walk out the door, merging into the hall traffic.

"I'm a method musician," Bree answers loudly over the din of the hallway.

"What does that even mean?" Deirdre calls over her shoulder.

"It's like method actors—how they stay in character the whole time they're shooting a movie or whatever. Something like that," Bree explains.

"So you're becoming one with your flute?" I ask.

"There are only a few days left before the audition for first chair. And you know they don't usually give it to seventh graders. If I'm going to stand a chance, I need to come up with a new technique. *This* is it," Bree says, lifting the end of her case into the air. Deirdre, Bree, and I all joined our elementary school band in fourth grade, but Deirdre and I were never serious about it like Bree was. We also were never very good. Which may have something to do with why the two of us quit band when we came to middle school last year.

I twist my *Tess* necklace around my index finger as we make our way toward our lockers. My parents gave me the necklace for my twelfth birthday, and it's pretty much my favorite accessory ever. Which is really saying something, because I do love accessories.

I hang on to the end of Bree's flute case as she shifts herself over to the side of the hallway where our lockers are, pulling Deirdre and me behind her like an off-the-rails train. I feel the bump of a foot under the sole of my shoe as Bree drags us through the crowd.

"Oops, sorry!" I call out to whoever I just squashed, looking around for the victim.

"Watch where your hooves are landing, Maven," I hear in response. Kate.

Sorry—Kayte. She added the *y* this year. As if that would make her more interesting.

"She said 'sorry,' Reynolds," Deirdre defends me.

"I really don't think I stepped on you that hard," I say. "But sorry if I did." I try to keep the peace with Kate—I mean, KAYTE—Reynolds more than Deirdre does. To me, she's not worth the aggravation. She always seems to want to argue, so why give her the satisfaction?

"Again with that necklace?" Kayte juts her chin out toward the chain around my neck. "You've worn that—what—three weeks in a row now? Someone's stuck in a rut."

"It's a classic," I explain.

"It went out in, like, 1997," Kayte says.

"I love it," I say, and shrug, trying not to let Kayte's criticism bother me. Kayte thinks of herself as being the top fashion plate of Twining Ridge Middle School. And sometimes even I have to admit that the outfits she puts together are pretty cool. Even if they're ugly, they're usually weird enough to catch your eye. Today, for instance, Kayte is wearing leggings that look like crocodile skin, and her legs are so long and wiry that they seem to go on forever. She's paired them with a loose-fitting white sweater on top, and it sweeps off her shoulder on one side, revealing a neon-pink tank top underneath. The tank top matches her shoes, which are simple ballet flats, only they're the color of a Barbie doll's nail polish. I would never, ever wear this getup, but it certainly makes Kayte stand out in the hallway.

Now, of course there is one huge problem with Kayte's ensemble, and that is that she isn't wearing a single accessory. Not even a stud earring, because— horror of horrors—Kayte's ears aren't pierced. And no outfit is complete without an accessory . . . or two or three or seventeen. At least that's what I say.

"You're blocking my locker." Bree's voice drifts back into my ear, and I snap out of my Kayte Reynolds wardrobe study.

"Sorry." I move to the side and begin twisting my own combination. Bree's, Deirdre's, and my lockers are all in the same wall block. By alphabetical fortune, Bree Laurence, Tess Maven, and Deirdre Noir almost always end up in the same homeroom.

And even more thankfully, Kayte Reynolds rarely does.

"Someone needs to push her off her high horse," Deirdre calls above the rapidly quieting hallway noise. If we don't speed it up, we're definitely going to be late for Pre-Algebra, and Mr. Dimmer never lets us off the hook like Ms. Castleby does. There's a reason we refer to him as the Dimmer Switch, after all. A sense of humor isn't really his strong suit.

"Just ignore Kayte," I say to Deirdre. "You only encourage her."

"Well, did you see how she was looking at my belt?" Deirdre asks. "It was as if I had a live rat tied around my waist."

"I did warn you about that belt," I say, slamming my locker shut and hurrying toward Mr. Dimmer's classroom. "Hurry up, or he's going to lock us out again."

"Brownnoser," Deirdre teases, but she walks in directly behind me, Bree and her flute following us. I slow down my pace as I reach my desk, because on the first day of school, Mr. Dimmer gave me the worst seating assignment of all of my classes—directly next to none other than the self-proclaimed fashion plate herself, Kayte Reynolds.

Chapter 2

I slide into my chair and glance over at Kayte, whose phone is so close to her face that it's making her look cross-eyed.

"What's so interesting there?" I ask.

"I don't recall addressing you," Kayte answers rudely, still not glancing up from her phone. I roll my eyes as far up as they will go, looking across the room to see if I can catch Deirdre's or Bree's glance. But Dimmer Switch assigned those lucky ducks seats next to each other, so they're already deep in conversation, leaving me to my own torture. The bell rings, and Mr. Dimmer pulls his classroom door closed with a slam, and locks it from the inside. If you're late to his class, he knows it, and he makes you suffer. No creeping in quietly with the sound of the bell around here. No, Dimmer leaves you out in the hallway to flounder for a full thirty seconds, which seems much longer when you're stuck in a silent corridor. And then, after he finally lets you in, he gives you extra homework. Not simple homework either—challenging word problems that will make your head spin.

I've only been locked out of Dimmer Switch's classroom once, and I've vowed to never let it happen again. Though, between Deirdre and Bree, they seem determined to help me break this streak every day.

Kayte places her phone on her desk while she roots around in her bag for a pencil—no pens allowed in Dimmer's class—and the screen is still open to what she was looking at. I recognize the logo across the top of the website instantly—Miscellaneous Moxie, my very favorite daily fashion blog. I read it religiously. Like some people read the Bible or celebrity magazines or the classics, I read Miscellaneous Moxie's daily musings on current fashion. Especially because, just like me, MM (which is what all of the fans call the site for short) is obsessed with accessories. That's what they write about the most, and they label each accessory-based post "TheBlingZone."

MM is where I heard about the antique-jewelry exhibition. The jewels have been circling the country for months, popping up in various cities for a few weeks at a time. The second I saw the advertisement for our local museum, I begged Mom to take me, which I realize now was a bad move. I should have pretended I wasn't that interested, because as soon as Mom figures out I really want something, she holds it over my head in the name of making me "more conscientious."

You would think by now that I would have caught onto this pattern and played it cool about the museum show, but sometimes my excitement about accessories overtakes me and I just can't help myself.

I don't usually read MM until after school—it's my reward for getting through the day—but with it right there, directly in front of me, I feel my eyes being drawn closer and closer to Kayte's screen. I'm stretching my vision to see what their post of the day is focused on, just a quick glance at—

Kayte's hand—her ringless hand, I might add—slaps down on top of her phone, covering the screen and turning it off in one swift motion, before depositing it into her bag. I run my hand through the front of my hair and let it fall to my right so that Kayte can't see my face. A strand flutters across my eyelashes, and I pick at the area blindly until I remove it, then I hold the hair out in front of me to examine. Even on its own, the strand stays in a soft wave, not straight but not exactly curly either, not blond but not exactly brunette. Mom won't let me get my hair dyed yet—not until my freshmen year of high school, she says—but the second I hit eighth-grade graduation, that is my first goal.

I flip my hair back to the other side of my face as Dimmer drones on at the front of the room about percentages. I wonder if Kayte dyes her hair. It's so blond that I would think she'd have to, but at the same time she's always had that hair color—so yellow that from a distance it's almost white. Similarly, Deirdre has always had her thick red lion's mane, Bree her stick-straight curtain of black. My hair needs a color. At this point I would settle for almost any color. Even the Barbie doll pink of Kayte's shoes.

"Miss Maven, are you with us back there?" Dimmer Switch's deep voice booms across our classroom, striking me out of my hair salon daydreams.

"Absolutely!" I call back, smiling widely at Dimmer, which seems to appease him. He pulls at his sports jacket by the collar, tightening it across his shoulders. Almost all of Dimmer's jackets have oval pads covering the elbow parts of the arms. Deirdre and Bree make fun of this mercilessly, but I kind of love them. They give his jackets, and therefore Mr. Dimmer himself, more personality than they would have otherwise. I wonder why girls' blazers never come with elbow patches. Or if they do, I've never seen them. Maybe I could start creating some of my own patches. My cousin Ava is a wizard with a sewing machine. I'm sure she could help me accomplish my elbow pad vision.

Although then, of course, Deirdre and Bree would start calling me Mini-Dimmer, or Dimmerer Switch, or Dimmer Switch II. But they just don't understand creative fashion choices like I do.

"Tess Maven!" Mr. Dimmer's voice startles me again, and I sit up straight in my seat with my hands folded on top of my desk.

"Yes?" I ask sweetly.

"Would you care to come complete this problem today, or do we have to wait until the Fourth of July?" he asks.

"Sorry," I say, hurrying up from my desk. "Wait, you want me to come up there, right?" I hear Kayte snicker. I really need to start paying more attention in this class.

"If you'd be so kind," Mr. Dimmer says, staring at me. I walk slowly to the board, examining the problem my whole way up. I look down at my fingers, longing for the days when they were useful enough math tools, before these x's and y's started ruining all the fun. It's only then that I notice it—the missing ring.

My infinity ring, the one I wear on my right pinkie finger. I just bought it two weeks ago, and it was a little loose, and Mom kept telling me not to wear it on my pinkie, but I insisted and—

"Oh no. No, no, no, no, no, no, no." I hear myself speaking, and feel my feet grind to a halt in the middle of the aisle, only halfway to the board.

"I— I think I— I need to—" I stammer, and I see Deirdre and Bree looking at me with concern from across the room. "Will you excuse me? Please, Mr. Dimmer. It's an emergency."

I start walking toward the door before he can answer, and his flustered "Very well, then" response makes me think that I must look like I'm going to be sick. I jog through the empty hallways all the way to the nurse's office. Not because I'm about to throw up, but because that's where the Lost and Found is located. I barge through the door and rush to the corner where the bins are kept, bypassing Mrs. Latara's questioning look.

"I just— I need to— I lost something," I explain without stopping. "Has anyone turned in a ring?"

"I don't police the Lost and Found, dear," Mrs. Latara answers curtly, and I hope I never have to go to her with a real medical problem, because she doesn't seem all that helpful. I dig through the bins one by one, quickly and then more carefully. Nothing. Even when my ring isn't in the box with the other lost jewelry, I look through every other container, just in case it got mixed up with something else.

Still nothing.

"What do I do now?" I ask Mrs. Latara, who is in the midst of sorting through a box of bandages, looking bored. "Like, is there a list somewhere in case someone turns it in?"

"What exactly are you looking for?" she finally asks.

"A ring," I say. "It's silver, and it has an infinity symbol across the top, and it's small because I wore it on my pinkie, and—"

"We don't keep a list for rings," Mrs. Latara interrupts me. "Just wallets and phones. Though, why you kids need to bring such things to school is beyond me, but that's an argument I've lost many times."

"So there's nothing I can do?" I ask, ignoring her anti-phone rant.

Mrs. Latara shrugs. "Like I said, I don't police the Lost and Found. But you can check back again tomorrow, I suppose. Sometimes things turn up."

"If I leave you my name, can you at least let me know if—"

"I only keep lists for wallets and phones," she repeats. "Like I told you."

I bite the insides of my cheeks—hard—to keep from tearing up. I know that it's just a ring. I get that it's not a matter of life and death and all that. But I hate to lose things. Anything. Particularly things I love.

Particularly things that Mom specifically warned me

I would lose if I didn't change the finger on which I was wearing it. So much for being conscientious.

I walk out of Mrs. Latara's office, calling a depressed "Thank you" over my shoulder. I head into the first girls' bathroom I see, which is luckily empty, and I dab at the corners of my eyes with a wet paper towel, trying to disguise the tears. But every time I lift a towel to my cheek, I see my hand with the ringless pinkie finger in the mirror, and it makes me upset all over again. I eventually just rest with my back against a wall and close my eyes until I can feel my face return to normal.

I leave the bathroom and begin to saunter down the hallway toward Mr. Dimmer's classroom, my eyes scanning the carpet back and forth all the way, studying it like a roving spotlight and looking for any signs of found infinity.

Chapter 3

I decide I can't go back into Dimmer's classroom now. I'd have to explain myself in front of the whole room, and that's pretty much the last thing I feel like doing. When I reach the seventh-grade hallway, I drag my toes across the carpeting one foot at a time, moving as slowly as possible. I kneel down to examine my boots, making sure that I'm not scuffing any red off the toes. I think about crawling along the hallway on my hands and knees to look for my ring more closely, but that just seems like a disaster waiting to happen. I glance at my watch—seven minutes until the end of Pre-Algebra. I crouch down and slide into the small space between Dimmer's door and the row of lockers along the wall, and I wait.

I twist around the jewelry on my right wrist—my watch, with different gemstones representing each number, a small beaded bracelet with a glimmering heart, and a bangle that has *Sparkle is my favorite color* written in cursive along its exterior. My right wrist accessories are almost always the same; since I'm right-handed, I need to make sure that I can write with whatever is on that wrist, and I'm used to this combination. My left wrist, though, changes almost every day. Sometimes I only wear one bracelet, sometimes five, sometimes even more. Sometimes they match, and sometimes I choose a variety. I am just about to examine my choices for today when the bell rings, and I leap to my feet before I'm smacked by Dimmer's door (and before he realizes that I've been hiding out here instead of returning to his classroom). I slip in as soon as one of my classmates exits, and I walk right over to his desk.

"I'm really sorry about that," I say sincerely when I reach him. I decide that the less information I provide, the better. Hopefully, Dimmer Switch won't ask for many details.

"Are you feeling better now?" he asks, a genuine look of concern in his gray eyes. Dimmer is really not so bad all the time, I guess.

"Much," I answer. "Thank you for your understanding."

"Glad to hear it," Dimmer says. "Is there someone in here who can fill you in on your homework for tonight?"

"Yes, Deirdre or Bree will," I tell him, backing toward

my desk slowly to grab my things. Thankfully, it looks like Kayte has already left.

"Good." He nods, ending our exchange. I pick up my stuff and meet my friends outside the room, where they are practically salivating with curiosity.

"What happened?" Bree screeches. "I was afraid you died."

"That's awfully dramatic," I tell her.

"Seriously, you looked like you had seen a ghost," Deirdre adds. "Explain yourself."

I hold up my hand with the empty pinkie finger. "I lost my infinity ring." I try to say this calmly, though I hear a faint quaver in the back of my voice.

Bree and Deirdre stare at me for a few moments without speaking, and I shoo them away from Dimmer's door before he can overhear us.

"Wait, that's actually the whole story?" Deirdre asks. "You lost a ring?"

"I love that ring!" I explain. "You know, it has the infinity symbol, like the number eight taking a nap. Plus, I just got it. I went to the Lost and Found to look for it, and nothing. I'm really upset."

"That's ridiculous," Bree says. "There's no need to get all crazy like that over a ring."

"You don't understand," I tell her. "You don't care about bling like I do."

"Bling? We're using 'bling' now?" Deirdre asks.

"That's what Miscellaneous Moxie calls . . . ," I begin, but then I stop myself. Deirdre and Bree won't understand, no matter how much I try. They both dress nicely enough, I suppose, but fashion really isn't their thing.

Though, they could still exhibit a little more sympathy about the infinity ring situation, if you ask me.

"I wasn't saying it's the end of the world," I tell them. "I was just saying the ring is important to me. Plus, my mom is going to be *so mad* if she finds out."

"Why would your mom be mad? Didn't you buy that ring yourself?" Bree asks.

"She'll say I wasn't being conscientious," I say with a sigh. "Because she told me not to wear the ring on my pinkie finger, and I wore it there anyway. Trust me."

"Then don't tell her," Deirdre says. "Just pretend the ring is buried in that accessory-hoarding place that you call a bedroom, and you'll be fine."

"But it's still lost," I say. "And I care that it's lost. I love that ring."

"There are people starving in the world, and you're moping about a ring," Deirdre says, teasing me. But I'm not in the mood for her snarkiness right now.

"You could at least pretend to care a little more," I tell them. "Fake it if you have to."

21

"Sorry, yeah, we stink as best friends," Deirdre says, throwing her arm over my shoulders. "You can sign up for some new ones if you want."

"Very funny," I say, moping down the hallway.

"I bet it turns up," Bree says. "Don't worry about it."

"Like you're not worrying about your audition?" I ask, now teasing her.

"That's different," she says, stroking her flute case like it's a cat. "We can help you find your ring after school. Right?" She turns to Deirdre.

"Sure," Deirdre agrees. "Or actually, no. I can't. I have . . . gymnastics."

"I thought that didn't start until after four," Bree says.

"What, are you the official keeper of my schedule?" Deirdre asks, her cheeks flushing a slight pink. "Sorry, Tess. You know I would, but I just . . . I can't today."

"What do you have to do right after school that we don't know—"

"No, it's okay," I cut Bree off. "I have to meet Mimi after school anyway. She's supposed to pick Toby up at the bus stop, and I just . . . I have to be there. Thanks, though."

"So we're forgiven for our lack of ring sympathy?" Bree asks.

"Yeah," I say. "But someone has to give me Dimmer Switch's homework assignment."

"Ugh, I was really hoping that after your little meltdown, he would forget to teach the rest of class," Deirdre says. "No such luck."

"There," Bree says, and I feel my phone buzz in my pocket just as she finishes typing furiously with her thumbs. "I texted you the homework. Let's get to Social Studies so we can wrap this day up once and for all." She links her arm around my elbow, and I link my arm around Deirdre's. We march down the hallway as a pack, but we can only make it a few feet before our chain is broken by a group of girls trying to get by, and my elbows are free again.

A flower pattern. That would make a nice elbow patch. A large, bright floral standing out on a crisp white jacket. That would be amazing. Maybe these two wouldn't even notice how much it resembled Dimmer Switch's sport coat style. . . .

Plus, maybe a couple of new elbow patches could help me forget about my missing ring.

"Mimi, I'm home," I call as I enter through the back door after school. "Mimi!"

"Here I am, Tessie," my grandmother says, coming around the corner from the kitchen. She takes my face in her hands and plants her pink lipsticked lips on mine. Mimi is one of the only people in the world who is

23

allowed to do two things—call me Tessie and kiss me on the lips. "How was your day?"

"Meh, it was fine," I tell her as we head into the kitchen. I throw my book bag onto the floor by the counter's edge and settle onto a stool. A large pot sits on the stove, and the comforting smell of warm broth drifts around the kitchen. "What are you making?"

"What was that?" she asks, lifting a wooden spoon off the stove.

"What are you making?" I repeat.

"Oh, what am I making . . . ," she begins, staring into the pot. "Let's see. A stew. For dinner."

"Sounds good," I tell her, even though I know Mom hates for Mimi to cook when none of us is home. I don't think it's my place to yell at Mimi about such things, and plus, I'm home now, and despite how irresponsible Mom and Dad seem to think I am, I'm pretty sure I can handle not letting the house burn down on my watch. "Remember, we have to pick Toby up from the corner in fifteen minutes."

"Is it that time already?" Mimi asks. "Where does the day go?"

"It goes pretty slowly at school, let me tell you," I say, and I take a banana from the bowl in the center of the counter and begin unpeeling it.

"How was your day?" Mimi asks again, and I pretend I haven't already answered this.

"I lost my ring," I confess. "You know, the one with the infinity symbol that I just got at Threads? It's gone."

"Oh no," Mimi says, turning away from stirring the stew to look at me sadly. "Don't worry. You can get another one."

"I saved more than a month's worth of allowance for that one," I say, shaking my head sadly.

"I'll buy it," Mimi says, waving her hand dismissively as if this is no problem. "Don't you worry, Tessie."

"You can't buy me a new ring, Mimi," I tell her. "Mom would kill me."

"Who said your mother has to know?" Mimi says, winking at me with her dark black lashes. Mimi is still one of the most glamorous people in the world, at least to me. Even if she has no plans to leave the house all day, she always gets fully dressed in the morning, with perfect hair and pretty makeup and a bunch of jewelry and everything. Sometimes she even wears a hat around the house, just for fun. Or a cape, or the little chunky heels that she loves. Plus, Mimi wears a different pair of dangly earrings every single day. I swear I don't remember ever seeing the same ones twice, though I'm sure I must have. Her hair is cut short, which makes her earrings stand out even more, and sometimes I think about cutting my own hair, just to see what it would look like.

"I'm not going to let you buy me the ring," I say to Mimi, not reminding her of the fact that my parents don't really let her keep any cash in her purse now anyway, let alone credit cards. "But thank you."

"You're too good a girl, Tessie," Mimi says, lifting the pot off the burner. "It's going to get you in trouble someday, all of that goodness."

"I'm not that good," I tell her, getting up to place my banana peel in the trash. "I skipped my entire pre-algebra class today to go look for my ring." I would never tell Mom and Dad this, but with Mimi I can be honest. Because besides being the most glamorous, Mimi is also the most honest person I know. "We should go soon," I remind her. "Toby's bus will be here in a couple of minutes."

"Oh, yes," Mimi says, brushing her hands across the front of her apron before untying it. "I'm all set." She grabs her purse off the counter and immediately heads out the back door. Quickly I turn off the stove, which she left on, and I take both of our jackets from the closet. I lock the door behind me when I leave and lift Toby's scooter from the porch. Then I follow the sound of Mimi's chunky heels down the driveway.

Chapter 4

Toby bounces off the last step of the school bus with a huge leap, and he almost lands on top of Mimi's toes.

"Easy there, my boy," she says, and hugs him, running one of her hands over the top of his buzzed hair.

"Scooter, please," Toby says when Mimi releases him, and he reaches his arms out toward mine.

"What do you say?" I prompt him, strapping his helmet around the faint freckles on his chin.

"I said 'please,'" Toby responds, his dark brown eyes looking up innocently into my own. Even though I'm less than five years older than him, sometimes it feels like he's at least a decade younger. Not that Toby is so terrible, really. He can actually be pretty fun, at least when he's listening.

"I meant 'Hi, Tess, my favorite sister,'" I remind him.

"You're my only sister," he says, handing Mimi his book bag as he climbs onto the scooter. Then he pushes off toward our house.

"That automatically makes me the favorite," I tell him. "Duh."

"This way, Toby," Mimi calls after him. "We're heading into town for a bit."

"For what?" Toby steps off his scooter but doesn't return to us.

"Yeah, for what?" I whisper to Mimi.

"We're going to stop by Threads," Mimi says, patting her purse.

"No, you really don't have to—" I begin, but Mimi cuts me off.

"We'll just look around," she says. "No harm in window shopping, right?"

I give Mimi a small smile. She probably hasn't left the house all day, so it's only right that we all get out for a bit. "Right," I answer. "Let's go, Toby!" Toby scoots ahead of us for the four blocks it takes to walk to the main street of our town, Twining Ridge Road, where a bunch of the shops and restaurants are located. This is one thing I love about where we live—you don't always need a car to get where you're going. Of course, there are a bunch of other places around the town that are too far to walk to, but for Mimi (who doesn't drive anymore), Toby, and me, Twining Ridge Road is the perfect place.

"Can we get ice cream?" Toby asks, which is what he asks every time we pass the ice cream shop.

"Not today," Mimi calls to him. "Maybe next time." Toby accepts this news without argument and continues rolling down the sidewalk.

"Wait!" I yell for him. "We're going to stop in here for a second." I look into Threads's wide front window, which they change to a new display every month. For a small store, Threads seems to have everything, and I'm pretty sure some of the most creative people in the world work there, because their front window is always gorgeous. This month, birds seem to fly across the windowpanes, sitting around the mannequins on display. When I look closer, I see that the birds are folded magazine pages, and they are "flying" from a thin white thread, almost invisible, that is woven like a spiderweb around the clothes in the window. I step away and stand on the curb to take a picture of the scene as Mimi walks through the door.

"Can't I just stay out here with my scooter?" Toby asks me. "I promise I won't leave the front of the store. Please?"

"Fine," I say. "But don't talk to anyone you don't know. Got it?"

"Got it good!" Toby answers, and he begins to scoot in a circle in front of Threads's window. I'm pretty sure he's going to be too dizzy to stand up straight by the time we get out.

I join Mimi inside the store and take a deep breath, inhaling the faint scent of hickory that is always present within Threads's walls. I run my hand over a shirt with soft silk cuffs, and another with fringe dangling off the pockets. But as much as I like Threads's clothes, it's their accessory section that really excites me. While most of the stuff on the clothing racks takes weeks' worth of allowance money to save up for, almost all of Threads's accessories are less than fifteen dollars. Many are even less than five dollars.

The infinity ring, however, was twenty-five dollars. Which is another reason it was special. Though, really, all of my accessories are special in some way. But that one was both special *and* expensive.

I find Mimi standing by the jewelry table, examining the rings. Threads keeps all of the rings on two huge life-like hands. It's as if someone took a mannequin but used it only from the wrists up, which sounds creepy, but at Threads it's not. They stack their ring selection on these ten fingers, all the way up to the fake nails, and I sometimes think about experimenting with layering some of my own rings on my fingers just like this.

"What kind of ring were you looking for again?" Mimi asks.

"I told you that you're not—"

"I know, I know," Mimi states. "No harm in seeing if they have another one, though, right?" I look up and down each finger of the mannequin hands, searching for the infinity symbol. I see every sort of gem, in all shapes and colors. I see gold-colored rings and silver-colored rings and rose-gold-colored rings and clear rings. Pointy geometric rings and soft spiral rings and thumb rings and pinkie rings and everything in between.

But no infinity ring.

"I don't see it," I tell Mimi.

"Can I help you two lovelies with something?" One of the Threads salesgirls approaches us.

"My granddaughter is looking for a ring she had that went missing. Tessie, what was it called again?" Mimi asks.

"An infinity ring," I answer. "It was silver, and very small, and it had an infinity symbol across the front, connecting the two sides."

"Oh, I remember that one," the salesgirl says. "No, unfortunately, I haven't seen that in a couple of weeks. We only get one or two of everything in the store, so things tend to sell out quickly." I nod, since I thought this would be the case. Even though I didn't expect to replace the ring today, it's sad to know that I may never be able

31

to. I walk over to the rack of scarves and begin sorting through them one by one, examining each pattern.

"Sorry I couldn't fix it," Mimi whispers into my ear from behind, and I lay my head on her shoulder with a smile.

"You don't have to fix it, Mimi," I tell her. "I'm a big girl."

"You'll always be a little girl to me," Mimi says. "Can I get you a scarf?"

"No, nothing today," I say. "Let's get Toby home before he throws up from dizziness." Mimi and I leave the store together, waving good-bye to the salesgirl, and begin the short walk home, with only the sounds of Mimi's shoes and Toby's wheels filling the air.

When we reach our house, I pick up my book bag from the kitchen floor and head down to the basement. No, not the basement—my room. My new room.

Mimi moved in with us just this past summer, so she took my old room, and I moved into the basement. It's not as scary as it sounds, or as dark and damp. It's kind of awesome, actually.

In fact, it's definitely awesome.

Mom and Dad made me my own "bedroom" down here, with all of my old furniture and everything, but that's not the real awesome part. The best reason for living in the basement is that there aren't any real closets, so I have a whole entire section of my room devoted to all of my fashions. Dad put together the clothes racks, which line one wall—shirts on one, skirts and dresses on another, pants on a third, and jackets on the last. My shoes are placed in pairs under each of these racks, sorted by season (flip-flops on one end, snow boots on the other) and then by color (from favorite to least favorite—purple, green, blue, pink, orange—just like my daily gel pens).

Across from all of these racks is the greatest part of my "closet"—a row of bookshelves with absolutely no books on them. Instead I've used them to display all of my accessories, organized by type and style. Bags take up one section, a few placed in each of the squares; jewelry is in the middle, with overflowing plastic boxes lining the little cubbies; belts and scarves hang from shower curtain hooks separating each shelf unit; and all of my hair and miscellaneous accessories are at the very end.

Mom and Dad like to say that if I would only spend as much time organizing my schoolwork as I do organizing my accessories, I would be on the honor roll. But social studies notes just can't hold a candle to the thrill that a perfectly arranged bracelet shelf gives me.

The other best part about my new bedroom is that at the back of this whole fashion section, against the wall under one of the small basement windows, sits a purple couch that Mom and Dad bought me as my "basement-warming" present. It's my go-to place to do my homework, even more than the desk that sits in the opposite corner. Because when I'm on this couch, I'm in the midst of all of my favorite things.

Which is also the best inspiration I can think of for completing Ms. Castleby's journal entries.

I slide my shoes off and into their proper place in line. Then I pad across the soft carpet barefoot and collapse onto the couch. I pull my phone out of my pocket and see a text from Bree: **Any luck with the ring?**

I stand and double-check my ring box, just to make sure I put it on today, though I'm certain that I did. I push around the rings, hoping by some miracle to see it, but it's not there. I return to my couch and type back to Bree, **Nope,** with a sad face.

Sorry, friend, she writes back.

Me too, I answer. I place my phone aside and pull my language arts journal out of my bag, along with my green Thursday gel pen. I glance around my beautiful fake closet and tap my pen against the front of my notebook. This little place of mine could really use a name, I think, so I turn to the back of the book and begin writing on the inside cover.

Accessory Castle. Boring.

Tess's Fashion Tower. Obnoxious.

Fortress of Fashion. Not bad, but not great.

I think about what would be the fanciest. What are some of the most sophisticated-sounding places in the world?

The Magic Kingdom. . . . The Taj Mahal. . . . Buckingham Palace.

Yes. A palace. What kind of palace? *Accessory Palace.* No.

Miscellaneous Moxie's favorite word pops into my head—"bling." *Tess's Bling Palace.* No.

Palace of Bling. Dumb.

Blingingham Palace.

YES.

It's kind of cheesy, maybe, but I sort of love it. I write it three times in a row on the back cover of my notebook, just to make sure: *Blingingham Palace, Blingingham Palace, Blingingham Palace.* Perfect.

This name also, of course, makes me the official, the esteemed, and the very royal Bling Queen.

Chapter 5

GLITTER: TO SPARKLE OR TO SHED—THAT IS THE QUESTION

I love glitter—I do. In small doses, it adds, well, sparkle to any outfit. It also just adds sparkle . . . to . . . everything. Your hair. Your lip gloss. The tip of your nose. Suddenly you're a life-size leaf-blower, only instead of spouting air, you spout glitter. You add shine to whatever you touch. Silver on the carpet, gold on your friend's sweater, rainbow on your test.

There are some people who wear glitter as part of their makeup. This, to me, is a gigantic no-no. Who wants to spend their days as a walk-around mirror ball? I promise you that there are ways to find your inner "glow" that do not involve covering yourself in actual shiny objects.

Then there are the glitter accessories. They seem like a good idea at the time, right? I mean, they're cute, they're fun, they give you the "pop" you're looking for. Only then you wear them, and KA-POW, you're a real-life Christmas card. You know how your parents hate those people who fill cards with confetti that then spills out all over your kitchen counter the minute you unseal the envelope? That is who you have become—a glitter monster.

Here's my tip with glitter: use the fake stuff. There are plenty of objects out there with what I call "faux glitter." It's glitter in disguise—teeny, tiny shiny objects that make you look like you're full of razzmatazz but don't actually make you full of razzmatazz. I have a pair of shoes that accomplishes just this function—from a distance, I'm parading around in heels stacked high with silver glitter, but up close, guess what? Just rhinestones. Miniature rhinestones that shimmer and shine and catch the light. And best of all?

They don't shed.

Once I finish the day's journal entry, I place the notebook next to me on my purple couch, keeping the pages open to make sure my gel pen doesn't smear. I get up to retrieve the rest of my pen pack from my book bag, and then I begin doing some mini-sketches in the paper's margins. I also write the word "glitter" in gigantic bubble letters at the bottom of the page, and I make soft polka dots onto the letters to make the word look like it's sparkling. I draw a picture of Deirdre's belt at the top of the left margin, and a picture of my non-glitter glittery shoes at the bottom. I'm not the best artist—my bubble letters are prettier than my illustrations—but I like adding some visuals to my journal. They make the whole thing more fun to look at.

I use the rest of my gel pens to underline and highlight some of the most important words in the entry, and then I step back and stare at it, seeing if it needs anything else.

And I must say that I'm pretty proud of the whole thing.

I pick up my phone and snap a photo of the entry, just like I have done for every journal page I've written. I file it into the correct picture folder on my phone, and then I flip through the photos quickly, looking for some of my favorite entries:

Overalls: Not Just for the Farmer in the Dell Anymore
Bibbidy Bobbidy Bobby Pins

Flannel: Still Not Back, Certainly Not Better Than Ever
Cuff Your Way Out of Fashion Jail
Bodysuit: The Ultimate One-Piece
Everyone's Inner Annie Oakley: Stirrup Pants

I rename the photo folder from "Journal Pics" to "BLING QUEEN." Then I decide to text Deirdre the picture of today's entry with the caption, **You inspired me,** including a winky face. Feeling accomplished, I reward myself by opening the Miscellaneous Moxie website. I slide my body down into the corner of my couch with my knees curled up to my chest, as if I'm about to hear my most beloved preschool picture book. I scroll and see a photo of a boot with a charm bracelet wrapped around the ankle portion. "Snowed-In Fashion: Ankle Bracelets for Winter," the headline reads, and I am instantly intrigued. I have a few ankle bracelets stacked in my jewelry boxes, but I've never worn them anytime but the spring and summer. This is a brilliant idea.

A text dings from Deirdre at the top of my screen. **Reynolds = HUGE poser** is all it says. I reluctantly tap away from MM's site to answer her.

Huh? I write back.

Look what she just posted on ExtraUniverse. Two words: fashion journal.

I open ExtraUniverse's page and scroll to my "Universe

of Acquaintance" list until I find Kayte's name. I click on it, and her profile appears before me.

At the top of her page is a photograph of an open notebook. A notebook that looks eerily similar to the ones we use as journals in Ms. Castleby's class. And on this page, besides Kayte's writing, are tiny illustrations, bubble letters, highlighted words, and underlined phrases. And color—so much color. Plus, in this entry, on the notebook's faint blue lines, Kayte's loopy handwriting reads, *Fake Glitter: It's Not What's for Dinner.* The caption below the picture says, *All set for Castleby's journal collection tomorrow! Signed, *Glitz Girl*.*

I feel warmth spreading up my neck and onto my face. Fury. Rage. Shock. I quickly call Deirdre, my fingers feeling too fluttery to type properly.

"Absurd, right?" she says to answer the phone. "She's totally posing you."

"Is that— Do you think that's how her whole journal is?" I ask. "It looks *just like* mine."

"I *know*," Deirdre says. "Hence why she's a poser."

"It's even worse, though," I continue. "How did she know that I did today's entry about glitter?"

"Clearly she stole your journal," Deirdre says. "It's the only explanation."

"She didn't steal my journal. I've never lost it," I say. "Plus, I just wrote that entry now." I take a deep breath.

"This is bad. This is bad, bad, bad. What if Ms. Castleby thinks I was copying Kayte? What if she thinks *I'm* the poser?"

"She won't. Castleby loves you," Deirdre says.

"But how is it possible that we both wrote about glitter on the same day? Ms. Castleby will definitely find that suspicious. I can't believe this is—"

"Wait, did you write specifically about my glitter belt? Seriously? It wasn't that bad," Deirdre interrupts me.

"No—well, yes, indirectly, but not really," I say. "I said faux glitter is better than real glitter, so it's completely the opposite of what Kayte wrote, but really, how dare she? She can't do this."

"She just did," Deirdre says. "Now we have to find a way to stop her. What do you want me to do? I could try to steal her journal tomorrow."

"Too risky," I tell her. "You can't go around stealing people's stuff. Especially not Kayte's."

"What if you just tell Castleby that you did the fashion journal idea first?" Deirdre suggests.

"I think that will make me look guiltier," I say. "Like I'm too defensive about it. I mean, Kayte used different-colored pens and drew pictures and did bubble letters and everything. Hers is *just like* mine."

"Only yours is way better," Deirdre says.

"You have to say that," I tell her. "This is a disaster.

I was working really hard on this, and now the whole thing could be ruined. What if Ms. Castleby makes me write the entire journal over again, with no fashion stuff? I don't like writing about anything else."

Toby bounds down the basement stairs and flops down onto the couch next to me, repeating the word "dinner" over and over, so loudly that I can't even hear Deirdre's response.

"Toby, I'm talking!" I yell at him, more harshly than I usually do, but I have no patience right now.

"It's DINNERtime!" Toby yells back, right into my ear.

"You gotta go?" Deirdre asks.

"I do," I say. "Sorry."

"No worries," she says. "I'll keep thinking about this poser situation. But I say you just hand in your journal and let Castleby see that all your fashion entries are superior. I mean, you're definitely her favorite anyway. She'd never believe Reynolds over you."

"I hope so," I say.

"DINNERTIME!" Toby laughs harder at himself every time he yells it. I try to place my hand over his mouth to stop him as I say good-bye to Deirdre, but he wiggles his tongue against my palm.

"Ew, Toby, stop it!" I say, wiping my wet hand across the carpet. "That's gross."

Toby picks a shower curtain hook off of the bookshelves and begins draping each of its scarves over his head. "I am Scarf Man. I've come to eat you for dinner." I grab him around the waist to tickle-tackle him, and he starts laughing uncontrollably as I dig my fingers into his armpits.

"You better watch it, Scarf Man, or Tickle Claws is going to ban you from Blingingham Palace," I tell him.

"Tess and Toby, are you coming?" Mimi's voice rings down from the top of the stairs.

"Yeah!" we call back, and I follow Scarf Man up the steps, leaving both messes—the pile of scarves and the copycatting Kayte Reynolds—behind me.

Chapter 6

Deirdre, Bree, and I meet at our usual corner of the seventh-grade hallway the next morning, and we huddle together in a pack to discuss our plan.

"Did you decide if you're going to talk to Ms. Castleby?" Bree asks. Immediately after getting off the phone with me last night, Deirdre filled Bree in about the whole journal situation.

"I'm not going to," I tell her. Bree places her flute case in between the two rubber soles of her sneakers in order to loop her dark hair into a ponytail. "You're still carrying that thing around with you everywhere?"

"Don't change the subject," Deirdre says. "So you're going to let Reynolds get away with copying your fashion journal idea?"

"I mean, I don't even know for sure that she copied

me," I point out. "Maybe she came up with that idea on her own."

"Oh, come on," Deirdre begins. "There is no way that happened. It looks *so much* like yours. Are you sure she didn't steal your journal out of your bag?"

"And then put it back before I noticed?" I say. "I don't think that makes sense."

"Stop shooting down all of my theories and concentrate on the problem at hand," Deirdre says. "And speaking of problems . . ." Deirdre thrusts her chin out, gesturing for Bree and me to turn around. Sauntering down the hallway, today in red pants with a leather strip running up each side, a plain white T-shirt, gold clogs, and a matching gold vest, is Kayte.

"She looks like a clown," Deirdre scoffs. "Look at that getup. Aren't metallics and leather together a huge no-no?"

The combination, while I wouldn't wear it, isn't really that bad. I mean, it certainly makes you look, which seems to be Kayte's entire mission in life. But it definitely needs some accessories to go with it. A long chain with a big charm as a necklace, a shiny gold cuff as a bracelet, a simple black leather headband—that would pull the whole look together.

"Tess, are you even paying attention?" The back of Bree's hand slaps against my wrist, pulling me out of my study. "Are you going to confront her or not?"

45

"Right. Yes, I am." I run my fingers through the front of my hair to fluff it, as if I'm putting on a helmet for battle. I walk straight up to Kayte, who has stopped to deposit her things in her locker.

And then I freeze.

"May I help you?" Kayte barely glances at me out of the corner of her eye, and I look over my shoulder at Deirdre and Bree, who nod encouragingly.

"I saw, um, that thing. That thing you posted," I begin, which I admit is not that intimidating of an opening line.

"What 'thing'?" Kayte asks in a mocking tone.

"Your journal," I say. "For Ms. Castleby's class."

"What about it? Jealous of my brilliance?"

"Um, no," I say. "You— I mean, it—well, it looks an awful lot like— Did you take that from—"

"Oh, for Pete's sake." Deirdre and Bree are suddenly on either side of me, standing like protection at each of my hips. "You copied Tess's journal, you poser," Deirdre launches in. "You took her fashion idea, and you copied it, because you're too lame to come up with any ideas of your own."

"Excuse me?" Kayte responds, slamming her locker door. "I didn't copy anyone. Let alone Tess Maven." She practically spits my name.

"What you posted on ExtraUniverse proves differently," Bree pipes up. "It looks exactly like Tess's journal, in the same style she's been using all year. And the same type of topics."

"Well, I have also been doing my journal like that all year," Kayte snaps. "So I guess *you* have been copying *me*."

"I have not!" I defend myself. "You know, it's super-shady that our entries look the same. Plus, we both wrote about glitter yesterday. Only, we said completely opposite things about it, of course."

"Probably because your friend here gave us both such stellar inspiration with her accessorizing," Kayte says, gesturing toward Deirdre. "Speaking of which, have you found your ring?"

I narrow my eyes at her, instantly suspicious. "How did you know about my ring?"

"Oh please," Kayte says, leaning her shoulder casually against her locker as if we were having a friendly chat. "Everyone and their mother knows about your stupid ring, the way you three were squawking about it in the hallway."

I glance from Bree to Deirdre, reading their expressions, and it's clear they're not sure they believe Kayte either.

"I really don't want to fight with you," I tell her. "But you make it awfully hard."

"Yeah, why don't you just leave us alone?" Deirdre adds.

"Leave *you* alone?" Kayte begins. "As I recall, you're the one who started this. Believe me, I would love to leave you all alone, you and your hideous, busy outfits."

"Like what you wear is so awesome?" Deirdre retorts. "Here's a tip: it's not."

"Okay, come on," I say, pushing both Deirdre and Bree away from Kayte. "We don't have to listen to this."

"Go ahead. Run away, Maven," Kayte calls after us. "Just like you always do. You never could stand up for what's right and admit when you're wrong. I learned that the hard way in fifth grade, didn't I? You'll never change."

I continue to walk toward our homeroom, forcing myself not to turn around. The three of us duck through the doorway.

"I honestly think you should tell Castleby what she did," Deirdre says before heading to her seat.

"That's really the only way to stop her," Bree adds, carrying her flute to her desk. I don't answer either of them as I slide into my chair. I merely stare at my hands, picking at my plum-colored nail polish and trying to ignore the sound of Kayte's words bouncing around in my brain.

I decide that the best way to forget about my Kayte problems is to distract myself with the missing ring situation, so I excuse myself during our science class to check the Lost and Found again. Nothing new seems to have appeared since yesterday afternoon, and Mrs. Latara isn't even interested in saying "good morning," let alone helping me search through the bins. I take the long way back to our classroom so that I can look around the hallways while they're empty. We hardly ever have to go into the sixth-grade wing anymore, so there's not really a need to look there, and I don't have any classes in the eighth-grade wing. So I concentrate my search on all of the common areas: the halls by the gym, the locker room, the cafeteria, the auditorium, the computer lab. But no matter how hard I scan, my infinity ring never appears, and I walk toward Science even more disheartened than I was earlier.

When I turn the corner, I look up to find Deirdre at the other end of the hall with her back to me. I would recognize that long red hair anywhere, so I begin to call her name, but then I realize she's talking to someone. I walk quietly heel-to-toe down the hallway until I can peer around her humongous mane to see who it is, just to make sure it's not a teacher. I'm hoping for Bree and not Mrs. Matchinski, or else she might start asking what took me fifteen minutes to go to the bathroom.

When my view isn't being blocked by Deirdre's hair, I peer over her shoulder to see who is with her. Rocco Votello. He's pretty much the smartest kid in our class. Did Mrs. Matchinski just assign them as new lab partners?

I begin walking faster to surprise Deirdre, and then I hear it. Whispering. But not just whispering—whispering with *giggles*. What could Deirdre possibly be whispering with Rocco about, let alone whispering *and* giggling? The boy is many things—smart, nice enough, not completely bad-looking. But funny? Highly doubtful.

"Hey," I call when I'm a few feet from the classroom door. Deirdre whips around, startled. "What're you two up to?"

"Oh, hi—what are you—nothing," Deirdre says in a rush. She tucks both sides of her hair behind her ears, which is what she does whenever she's nervous.

Nervous?

I raise my eyebrows at her, silently asking for the real answer to what's going on, but Deirdre only breezes past me to the door.

"We all better get back inside before Matchinski freaks out," she says, and she hightails it to her lab stool faster than I've ever seen Deirdre enter Science.

And, among the many mysteries of my day—what happened to my ring, how Kayte figured out how to copy my journal, and what is up between Deirdre and Rocco Votello—at the moment, the last one is definitely the most intriguing.

Chapter 7

At the end of class Deirdre manages to run out before Bree and me, calling something over her shoulder about having to go to the bathroom. I walk over to Bree's lab table, deposit my purple gel pen—my Friday favorite—in my pocket, and wait for her as she gathers her things.

"So I saw Deirdre in the hallway . . . ," I begin in a low voice.

"Yeah?" Bree asks impatiently, as if I'm telling a very boring story. But she has no idea what's about to hit her.

"Whispering with Rocco Votello . . . ," I continue.

"Yeah?" Bree asks again as we walk out the classroom door, my books in my arms and her flute case in hers.

"But not just whispering—whispering *and* giggling," I say. "What is that about?"

"I have no idea," Bree answers. "I mean, Deirdre and Rocco could not have *less* in common."

"Right?" I say. "Are they lab partners now or something?"

"No, we didn't get new lab partners," Bree says. "Maybe they're . . . friends?"

"Please," I begin. "Deirdre never makes new friends. Not real friends anyway—not like us. She's definitely the least friendly of the three of us."

"Maybe she's turning over a new leaf," Bree says with a shrug.

"You don't think she likes Rocco, do you?" I ask. "Like, *likes* Rocco?"

"Ew, no way," Bree says. "Maybe they were just whispering about—"

"Whispering and giggling," I correct her.

"Whispering and giggling about . . ." Bree trails off. "Nope, still can't figure out a single thing they'd have to say to each other."

I pull my books closer to my chest as Bree and I weave down the packed hallway silently. At the very least Deirdre somehow managed to get my mind off my missing ring and my copied journal for a few minutes.

Not that it's making me feel any better about my day.

Bree and I don't have a chance to ask Deirdre about Rocco until we are all gathered around our table in the cafeteria.

We always sit in the same spot—third table on the right, all the way against the wall. Deirdre and I sit on one side, and Bree (and her flute case) on the other. Deirdre always buys her lunch, Bree brings hers, and I rotate between the two. But no matter what, Deirdre grabs extra containers of ketchup for us, because ketchup goes well with more things than people give it credit for.

We truly have our lunchtime routine down to a science.

I have brought my lunch today, so I sit with Bree and wait for Deirdre to return with her tray.

"We're going to confront her about this Rocco thing, right?" Bree asks.

"Well, we don't have to confront her," I say. "We can just ask."

"Same thing," Bree says. "Here she comes." Deirdre places her tray on the table next to me and sits down on the bench, swinging both legs around at the same time like a spinning top. The tip of her untied sneaker hits me in the arm.

"Hey, ow!" I yell. "You're supposed to be the graceful one, you know."

"Sorry," Deirdre says. "Any more run-ins with the Reynolds monster today?"

"Not yet," I say. "But we have Ms. Castleby next period, so we'll see how that goes."

"Okay, okay, enough with the small talk," Bree says.

"I don't really think that was small talk, but—" I begin, but Bree waves her hand to shush me.

"What were you doing with Rocco Votello in the hallway during Science?" Bree asks Deirdre.

Deirdre turns to me and stares. "You told her? Wow, it wasn't even a big deal."

"You seemed awfully whispery," I say. "And giggly."

"So?" Deirdre asks, tucking the sides of her hair behind her ears. Nervous.

"What is it, do you like him or something?" I ask. I try to make this last part sound like a joke, because there is no way Deirdre can like Rocco, right? What do they even have in common? Deirdre is smart enough, I guess, but Rocco is genius-level. And he doesn't seem to be the type who likes to walk around the block, let alone do gymnastics like she does.

"No," Deirdre says coldly. "I was just talking to him. Is talking not allowed now?"

"You were whispering, like you didn't want anyone else to hear," I say.

"Plus, you never talk to anyone except us," Bree tells her. "I mean, not really. Like a full-on conversation."

"That's not true," Deirdre protests. "You don't see who I talk to when I'm not with you."

"Because you're always with us," I point out. "Or with your gymnastics girls. But mostly us."

"You make it sound like I'm some kind of snob," Deirdre says defensively. "I talk to other people."

"Then why did you run away so quickly when I saw you with Rocco?" I ask her.

"To be clear, I didn't 'run,'" Deirdre says, snippier than normal. "I walked briskly."

"You scampered," I say. "And since when are you eager to get to Science?"

"Forgive me for trying to save us all the wrath of Matchinski," Deirdre says. "And honestly, is it such breaking news when one of us talks to another person?"

"It's not that you were talking to another person; it's that you were talking to Rocco," I explain. "It just seems like an odd choice. What do you two even have in common?"

"Why, am I not smart enough to talk to Rocco?" Deirdre asks.

"You know I would never say that—" I start.

"But it's what you meant," Deirdre persists, her dark eyes staring into mine in a way I don't recognize. She's really mad. This conversation is getting out of hand quickly.

"No, you're putting words into my mouth," I say

calmly. "I was just wondering how you two became friends."

"It's none of your business," Deirdre says.

What is up with her?

"You must like him," Bree says. "There's no way you'd be getting so crazy right now unless you had a crush on him."

"I. Don't. Have. A. Crush. On. Rocco," Deirdre insists. "We are friends. I'm allowed to have friends who aren't the two of you."

"But it makes it weird when you don't tell us about your new friends," I explain. "When you're secretive about it. That's why we're asking you."

"And I still don't understand *how* you're friends," Bree agrees. "And how you became friends in the first place."

"We've known Rocco forever," Deirdre says. "It's not like he's a stranger."

"But you've never been friendly with him before," Bree points out.

Deirdre shrugs. "You two don't know him. He's a really nice guy." The three of us sit quietly for a few moments, each lost in our own thoughts. I don't care that Deirdre has a new friend, not really.

But I *do* care that she is being super-shady about the whole thing.

"Didn't he throw up during reading time in second grade? I think I remember that," Bree says, interrupting our silence, and this memory makes me laugh. Loudly.

"That's right!" I say. "And they had to send Mr. Stan, the custodian, in to clean it up. The whole room smelled like popcorn." I hold my nose just at the memory of it, which now makes Bree laugh hard too.

"Seriously? That was *second grade*," Deirdre says, her face flushed with annoyance. "You're really going to hold something that happened in second grade against him?"

"Well, it's still gross," Bree says. "And why are you being so defensive about him? Unless you really do have a crush on him." She tries to say this last part jokingly, but Deirdre is having none of it.

"For the last time, I don't have a crush on Rocco," she says. "I just don't think you two should be making fun of him. You don't even know him."

"We're not making fun of him. Really," I tell her. "We can't help it that it's a fact that he threw up popcorn in second grade." This comment makes Bree laugh hard all over again, which only seems to make Deirdre angrier.

"Sorry. We'll stop," I say, wishing for peace to return to our table. "Let's just drop the whole thing, okay? And go back to having a normal lunch." Bree nods in agreement before taking a giant bite of her sandwich and then making a face. She moves her hand around as if looking

57

for something to dunk the sandwich in. "Hey, where's our ketchup?"

"I forgot it," Deirdre says curtly. She swishes her macaroni and cheese around in her bowl, but she never lifts the fork to her lips. Clearly my attempt to put this conversation behind us hasn't worked.

"Look, if you're friends with Rocco now, that's fine," I begin.

"Of course it's fine!" Deirdre yells. "We're allowed to have other friends, you know!"

"We never said we weren't," Bree pipes up. "We just think it's weird you didn't tell us."

"Whatever," Deirdre murmurs under her breath, and she continues to shift her pasta from one side of the bowl to the other. She pulls her phone out of her pocket and begins scrolling across the screen, her face turned away from us. I look across the table at Bree, and she shrugs.

"I'm going to get ketchup," she announces, but only I nod in response. Deirdre's head stays turned away from me, so I pull my own phone out of my bag and open Miscellaneous Moxie's page, because if there's anything I need right now, it's to be cheered up. At the very top of the page is a banner that reads, in fancy text bubble letters, *BLING CONTEST*. I click on it immediately, the tips of my fingers prickly with anticipation.

Have a fantastical idea for the newest, hottest piece
of bling?
We are now accepting entries for Miscellaneous
Moxie's first annual BLING CONTEST.
Here's your chance to design some bling of your
very own! Scroll down for details.

"Look at this!" I say, my eyes still focused on the screen. "This is amazing. I can't believe—" I reach my hand out to show my phone to my friends, but Deirdre has disappeared from the table, and Bree still hasn't returned with the ketchup. I feel a tiny knot form deep within my neck. But not even sitting at a cafeteria table alone can take away my excitement at possibly being an accessory designer for Miscellaneous Moxie.

At least, it can't completely take away my excitement. But it can take it away a little bit.

Chapter 8

Deirdre is already sitting at her desk when Bree and I arrive in Ms. Castleby's classroom. She is rolling strands of her hair into curls around her index finger while looking straight ahead at the board. Only, there isn't anything written on the board, so she's not really looking at it at all.

She's just *not* looking at us.

I tried to explain the MM contest to Bree as we walked down the hallway, but it was too noisy for her to hear me, and after I spotted Kayte behind us, I was too afraid of her eavesdropping to talk any louder. Not that I think she would actually enter an accessory design contest. It's not like she ever wears any, so she better not. But if Kayte heard I was interested in it, she might do it for spite, just like she copied my journal style.

"Place your journals in a neat pile next to my desk, please," Ms. Castleby calls as the rest of our class files in. If I'm going to say anything, now is the time, before she realizes how closely Kayte's and my journals resemble each other. I approach her desk, journal in hand, and try to think of what to say.

"Hi there," she greets me, glancing up from rearranging another class's pile of journals. "I'm looking forward to reading yours."

"Yeah, about that . . . ," I begin. "So I kind of did mine like a fashion journal, sort of thing. With each entry on a different trend, or object, or whatever. And I tried to make it look fancy with different colors and stuff and—"

"Sounds great," Ms. Castleby cuts me off. She walks out from behind her desk, and I notice then that her stockings today are sheer black with tiny hearts splattered all the way up her legs. They kind of look like something a five-year-old would wear.

They also kind of look amazing.

"Wow, I love those," I tell Ms. Castleby sincerely. She looks around the room like she's not sure what I'm referring to, and I point to her ankles.

"Oh, these," she says. "Yeah, I thought they were fun."

"Where did you get them?" I ask.

"There's this little boutique on the main drag—Threads," Ms. Castleby says. "They have some cute things."

I open my eyes wide in shock. "I adore Threads," I tell her. "It's pretty much my favorite place ever."

"That doesn't surprise me," Ms. Castleby says with a smile. "I can tell you like your accessories." She walks to the front of the room before I can say anything else about the journal, or Kayte, or Threads. I reluctantly place my journal in the pile with the rest of my classmates' and return to my seat.

"Hey." I tap Deirdre on the back with my purple gel pen. "Are you really not going to speak to me all day now?"

"Stop tapping me," Deirdre says instead of answering my question, and she keeps her face forward. I look across the room at Bree, who only raises her eyebrows.

As soon as the bell rings, Ms. Castleby begins handing sheets down each of our rows. When it's Deirdre's turn to pass to me, she tosses the remaining three papers over her head, and they flutter to the floor.

"Real nice," I whisper as I get up to gather them, but Deirdre ignores me. I sit back down and pass the rest of the sheets to the person behind me, who just happens to be Rocco Votello. I feel myself glaring at the top of his head, just because he's the one who caused this entire mess.

"As you can see here," Ms. Castleby begins, "I've

outlined what your assignment is in relation to your business plan projects. Over the weekend I'd like each of you to come up with a business idea that you think is needed—in your home, this school, our town, the world, whatever you prefer. You'll have time early next week to talk and brainstorm your ideas in small groups— everything from the concept itself to marketing to pricing and anything else that you think applies to your business. And then on Friday you'll each present your pitch to your classmates. Of course, this is a simple approach to business planning—real entrepreneurs take more than a week to pull their ideas together— and this project doesn't include all of the necessary business elements, like creating a budget and whatnot. But that math stuff isn't really Language-Arts-related anyway, right?"

"Thank goodness," I whisper for Deirdre's benefit, before remembering that she seems to have put a sound barrier up between our desks.

"Now, I'm sure you have questions, so let's hear them. Read over the sheets in front of you for a couple of minutes, and then we'll discuss together," Ms. Castleby says. "I'm just going to organize your journal pile while you read. We seem to have a Leaning Tower of Pisa situation going on back there."

I try to concentrate on the words written on the paper

in front of me, but my head feels swampy from the day. I consider asking Ms. Castleby if I can be excused to go to the Lost and Found, but I don't really feel like dealing with Mrs. Latara again. Plus, I'm almost 100 percent sure my ring won't be there.

I try to think of something I can write on a note to Deirdre—something that will make her laugh so that we can smooth over this entire situation. But my mind draws a blank, and I suddenly don't know what to say to the person with whom I have never run out of things to talk about before.

After all, it's kind of hard to be best friends with someone who's not speaking to you.

Usually by the time I get home on Fridays, I am giddy with happiness to have a whole weekend in front of me. But today I mope. I mope in the front door and greet Mimi in the living room. I mope with her to Toby's bus stop. I mope next to them on the way home. And then I try to mope into my basement bedroom to be mopey all by myself.

"Just a second there, Tessie," Mimi calls after me. "You're looking awfully lemony today."

"Lemony?" Toby calls as he grabs a handful of cereal out of its box, spilling at least seven kernels onto the floor in the process. "She's not even yellow!" He laughs loudly at his own joke, as if it's the funniest thing that's ever been said.

"Toby, how about you give your sister and me some girl time for a few minutes?" Mimi suggests.

"Can I ride my scooter?" Toby asks.

"Stay on the driveway only," Mimi instructs.

"And wear your jacket," I call after him as he bounces out the back door, trailing cereal crumbs behind him. Mimi takes a seat at the kitchen table and pats the chair next to her.

"Tell Mimi all your troubles," she says, and I think about where to start.

"Well, you know I lost my ring," I begin.

"Oh no!" Mimi exclaims, as if she hasn't heard this before. "Which one? I know how you love your rings."

"The one with the infinity symbol," I tell her again. It's no use reminding her that we went to Threads yesterday to look for a new one. That will only make her feel bad.

"You're upset that you lost your ring? I'll buy you a new one," Mimi says. "Here, we can go into town right now. Grab your coat." She begins to rise from her seat.

"No, Mimi, it's fine," I say, placing my own hand on top of hers gently. "Let's talk about something else. There's this project I have to do for school, and I could use your ideas."

"Okay, then," Mimi says, taking her seat again. "What is this project?"

"We have to come up with a business idea—a business we think is needed, and that we could maybe do ourselves," I explain. "We don't actually have to start running the business, but we have to come up with a solid plan and pitch it to our class next Friday."

"I love this!" Mimi exclaims. "Is this for that class you like? With your favorite teacher?"

"Yes," I answer. "For Language Arts. Ms. Castleby." It always surprises me what Mimi seems to remember, and then what she doesn't. How does she remember about my favorite teacher, but she can't recall that we went to Threads yesterday?

"Tell me more," Mimi continues, snapping me back to attention. "What are you thinking of doing?"

"Well," I begin. "At first I thought I could try to revamp the Lost and Found system at our school, because it's atrocious. But that doesn't really seem like much of a business. I mean, the best I could come up with is charging people to return their things, like a reward, so that people actually want to help others find their stuff. But that doesn't seem like a great idea."

"But it's not a terrible idea," Mimi says kindly. "I bet you could turn it into something that makes more sense for you. Think big, though. What would you do

66

as your dream job, if you could do anything in the world?"

"Design accessories," I answer instantly, without even thinking. "Actually, there's this contest that my favorite fashion site is sponsoring. You enter by sending your design idea for a brand-new accessory item. I think I want to enter."

"You should definitely enter," Mimi tells me. "What's your idea?"

"Okay. . . . Tell me if this sounds dumb," I say, lifting my *Tess* necklace off my chest with one finger, and pointing with my other hand at Mimi's dangling earrings. "I was thinking of nameplate earrings. I mean, these necklaces have been around for a while, but I've never seen names on earrings."

"I like it," Mimi says. "I think that could be lovely."

"Plus," I continue, feeling encouraged, "instead of just having the names written horizontally, like normal, what if they hung down, one letter on top of the other? So for my name, the *T* would be closest to my earlobe, with the *E*, *S*, and *S*, hanging below it. That would make the earrings dangly."

"Ooh, I like that even more," Mimi says. "You know my feelings on dangling earrings."

I laugh at this. "I certainly do," I say. "So maybe I could do two things at once—a design of these earrings for the contest, and then a business plan to sell them?"

"Sounds like a great place to start," Mimi says. "Feeling better now?"

"Yes," I say. "Much. Thanks." I kiss Mimi on the cheek as I stand to head to my room and get started.

"That's what I like to hear," Mimi says. "Now I'm going to go make sure your brother hasn't killed all the grass outside with that scooter of his." Mimi and I head off in different directions, and I bound down the basement steps, feeling much more positive about everything than I did all day. Maybe I could even call Deirdre now and settle this argument once and for all. She can't possibly hold this grudge against Bree and me forever.

I retrieve my phone and press Deirdre's name, and it rings four times with no answer. I hang up without leaving a message and pull a pad of paper off my desk. I bring the paper and my gel pens to my purple couch and settle down to begin sketching, burying my silent phone deep into the cushions and out of my mind.

Chapter 9

By the following morning I have plenty of sketches of my Miscellaneous Moxie bling contest entry, but not a single returned call or text from Deirdre. She's still not speaking to Bree, either, but Bree is convinced she will get over it by the time the weekend wraps up. I hope she's right. The three of us have definitely had spats before, but they've never lasted all that long. Maybe a few days, max. So Deirdre has to forgive us soon. . . .

Right?

When I open the basement door to pad into the kitchen for breakfast, I hear a faint tap against the wood. I peer around and find a necklace hanging off the doorknob—a solid gold chain with a plain heart-shaped charm dangling from the middle. I lift it off the knob and peer at it curiously before continuing into the kitchen. Mom is standing over the stove, scrambling eggs, and Mimi sits at the table, thumbing through the newspaper while sipping coffee.

"What is this?" I say as a greeting.

"Good morning to you, too," Mom responds. "What is what?"

"This." I hold the locket up in the air so they both can see.

"Oh, that," Mimi says. "That's for you, Tessie."

"Um, thank you," I begin, confused, and I look back and forth between the two of them. Mom is staring at Mimi like she also has no idea what Mimi is talking about. "What is it?"

"It's a locket, silly," Mimi tells me. "Bring it here. I'll show you." I walk over to the table, and Mimi takes the necklace from me. With her red-painted thumbnails, she pries open the heart, revealing the inside. A black-and-white picture is resting on either side of the heart, one more faded than the other, and I peer in for a closer look.

"Is that you?" I ask, pointing to a blurry image of a girl who looks about my age.

"Indeed," Mimi states. "And this is my grandmother—your, let's see now . . . your great-great-grandmother. She gave this locket to me. And now I give it to you." She hands the chain back to me, the heart still dangling open. "You know, also to cheer you up about the . . ." Mimi points to her own pinkie finger but doesn't say "infinity ring" out loud so that Mom doesn't catch on.

"Wow, thank you," I say, looking quickly at Mom to see if she is going to put an end to this, chalking it up to one of Mimi's "episodes." But Mom merely tilts her head quizzically at both of us.

"I guess that little heirloom skipped a generation, huh?" she asks Mimi, but there is a smile on the edges of her lips, teasing.

"Grandmother to granddaughter, dear," Mimi states. "We should probably update those pictures though." Mimi points to the inside of the locket. "To you and me, Tessie."

"I think I'll leave it with you two for now," I say, shutting the heart with a click and draping the chain around my neck. I run over to the hallway mirror and examine my reflection, and then I jog back down the basement stairs to retrieve something. I clasp my *Tess* necklace around my neck, and it hangs about an inch above the top of the heart—the perfect necklace layer. I return to the kitchen and model the combination for Mimi and Mom, asking what they think.

"Divine," Mimi states, nodding with satisfaction. "They look pretty together."

"They do," Mom says. "But, Tess, maybe you should

give the locket to me for safekeeping." She holds out her hand.

"Why? I want to wear it," I say.

"You know that's a family heirloom," Mom explains. "If you lose it, you can't just pop down to Threads and get another one. And with your track record . . ." Mom trails off, but her message is clear.

"I don't lose stuff," I say, more grateful than ever that Mom hasn't found out about the lost infinity ring yet. "I mean, I don't lose any more stuff than normal people lose."

"With the number of trips I've made with you to Threads to replace some must-have accessory you misplaced, I beg to differ, my dear," Mom says.

"That only happened, like, three times," I say. "And I was younger then. I'm more responsible now. More . . . *conscientious*." I give Mom a big grin at this word, hoping she'll get my point, and she smirks in return.

"That grade on your last social studies test would indicate something else," Mom says. "I really think you should leave the locket with me, and I'll give it back to you for Hayden's wedding next week. For now it should be a special-occasion accessory only."

"No, please," I beg. "I want to wear it today, and every day. I promise I won't lose it. Really. I hate to lose stuff. Please. Mimi?"

"Keep it on, Tessie," Mimi says. "It suits you."

Mom sighs. "You two make quite the dynamic duo, you know that?" she says. "If that's your decision, Tess, fine. But just know that if that locket goes missing, the consequences are going to be a lot more severe than not getting to go to a jewelry exhibition."

"So you're definitely going to take me to that, right?" I say, happy for an opportunity to change the subject. "It's only a few weeks away."

"Like I said before, we'll see," Mom says. "Let's see how you do over the next month with your schoolwork, and around the house. Maybe if you started spending less time organizing your accessory shelves and more time on real work . . ."

"But fashion is—" I begin, but then I stop myself. "Okay," I answer instead. "I'll prove that I deserve to go." It's no use arguing with Mom when she thinks she's right, so better to just tell her what she wants to hear.

"Now why don't you run and brush your teeth and all that before your brother and father wake up. Remember, you, me, and Mimi are heading to Uncle Peter's and Aunt Rebecca's right after breakfast. Last-minute fittings for the wedding and whatnot."

"You mean to *Ava's*," I correct her. "Can't wait." I run out of the kitchen to get ready quickly. Ava is only a year and a half older than me, and besides Bree and Deirdre, she's really my best friend, even though she's also my cousin. After all, I've technically known her the longest.

Plus, when half of your best friend circle isn't speaking to you, it's pretty comforting to have a best cousin for backup.

I am out of the backseat and up Ava's driveway before Mom has even turned off the car's engine. I punch the code for the garage door into the side panel, and I wait for the door to rise.

That's how you know you're close to someone—when you not only enter their house through the garage, but you also punch in the code yourself. I'm not sure even Mom and Mimi know the code, but I do. Ava taught it to me years ago, for just these kinds of moments.

"Tess, did you just let yourself in?" Mom calls after me, but I am through the garage and knocking on the inner door before I can answer her. I open it myself and walk past the laundry room and into the kitchen. I quickly greet Uncle Peter and Aunt Rebecca, then I dart up the stairs to Ava's bedroom.

Ava and I wiggle the tips of our fingers against each other's, which has been our "secret" greeting since I was almost seven and she was eight. Her older brother,

Anderson, used to make fun of us about it, and he even taught it to Toby so they could mimic us anytime we all get together. But Toby is home with Dad, and Anderson is off at college now, so we're safe to act like elementary schoolers if we want to.

"Did you finish it yet?" I ask, flopping down face-forward onto Ava's bed, where it seems like a thousand pieces of fabric are strewn across her pillow. Aunt Rebecca is an amazing seamstress, and Ava seems to have inherited her mom's talent for sewing. Aunt Rebecca mostly makes short jackets, and Ava sticks to scarves. But everything they create is lovely.

"Almost, but I want to fit it on her first," Ava says, lifting one end of a gorgeous new scarf and holding it up in the air. "Do you think Mimi will like it?"

"No, she'll love it," I say. "Does it match the jacket your mom is making for her?"

"Yep," Ava says. "Well, it's not an exact match, because that would be monotonous, but it has the same themes in it." I nod my head and remember one of the reasons I enjoy Ava so much: she's the only one who really seems to care about fashion the same way I do. Of course, she mostly cares about scarves right now (Aunt Rebecca says she's going through her "Scarf Period"), and I like all sorts of accessories, but still. Ava gets it, more than Deirdre or Bree ever will.

"It's beautiful," I assure her. "Did you make one for yourself, too? For the wedding?"

"Nah," Ava says. "I got a new dress, and it's really intricate up here." She gestures just under her neck and around her shoulders. "So I don't want to hide it with any scarf nonsense."

"Ooh, let me see it," I say. "I got a new dress for the wedding too. It's blue, which you know is only my third-favorite color, but whatever." I sit up straight on the bed with my legs crossed, watching Ava walk toward her closet.

"Wait, it's blue?" Ava asks. "What color blue?"

"Um, I don't know," I say. "Give me some options."

"Baby blue, sky blue, navy blue, teal, turquoise, cornflower blue, neon blue," Ava lists them off the top of her head—proof of how much time she spends studying fabric colors.

I think for a second. "It's like a mid-blue, almost purple-like," I say. "But not—what's the color?—periwinkle. It's not *that* purple. But it has a purple sheen to it." I think this is a pretty accurate description. "I got it at Threads—you know that store I've brought you to? Mom bought it for me, since Hayden's wedding is a special occasion and all that." Hayden and Harper are our older cousins, the daughters of Mom's and Uncle Peter's other brother. They're identical twins, and to this day Ava and

I can almost never tell them apart, even when we're with them. Harper could very easily walk down the aisle next weekend instead of Hayden, and we wouldn't know the difference.

"Is it this color?" Ava asks, whipping a plastic-enclosed dress out of her closet. "Cornflower blue?" The dress has a crisscross pattern, like the top of a pie, right under the collar, and it's fitted tightly in the waist, before flaring out at the bottom.

It is also the exact same color as the dress I bought for the wedding.

"Wow, yes!" I exclaim. "That color is pretty much identical to mine! Funny, huh? I guess Hayden and Harper won't be the only twins at the wedding."

Instead of laughing about this, like I expect her to, Ava looks at me blankly. "I really don't think we can wear the same color," she states.

I think for a moment, trying to figure out if she's kidding, but there's not even a hint of a smile on her face. "Why not?" I ask. "You don't think it's an amazing coincidence that we bought the same color? We should just run with it."

Ava sighs, redistributing the plastic over the dress and placing it back in her closet. "Fine," she says. "But we can't look exactly the same, or that will be really weird. What jewelry are you wearing?"

"I haven't decided yet," I say, unsure why Ava is being so serious about all of this. "But definitely my *Tess* necklace, and this locket from Mimi."

"Mimi gave that to you?" Ava asks in surprise. "Let me see." She kneels next to me on the bed and peers intensely at the heart around my neck. "Why did she give it to you?"

"Well, I lost this ring I liked, so she felt bad, and plus I'm entering this contest on Miscellaneous Moxie and she thought this would be good luck, so—"

"So you lost something and she rewarded you?" Ava asks, and she sounds awfully mean about the whole thing, for someone who's supposed to be my best cousin. "Typical." She says this last part under her breath—but just loudly enough for me to hear.

"What does that mean?" I ask. "Her grandmother gave it to her, and she thought I would like it."

"I'm her granddaughter too, you know," Ava points out, and she begins brushing her hair, which is the same color as mine, only with blond highlights sprinkled throughout—the exact shade I want to have the moment eighth-grade graduation is over. "You don't have to get everything."

"I don't get everything," I say.

"You do," Ava argues. "Especially since she moved in with you guys. It's different. She spoils you, and I just don't think it's fair. That's all." She shrugs. And even though she says "That's all," I can tell it's really "not all."

"I don't know why you're being so testy about this," I say. "First the dress, and now the locket?"

"Exactly," Ava says, placing her brush back onto her bureau. "I'm the one who taught you about fashion stuff to begin with, but now you're copying my outfits and getting Mimi's jewelry, just because you're right under her nose all the time."

"That's ridiculous. I didn't copy you—I didn't know what color dress you were wearing. And about Mimi, you're making a big deal out of nothing," I tell her, but Ava picks up Mimi's half-finished scarf and walks out before I can continue.

"It's a big deal to me," she calls over her shoulder, leaving me alone in her room.

First one best friend down, and now one best cousin.

Chapter 10

So Harper is Hayden's maid of honor, right?" Mom is asking when I join the rest of my family in the kitchen. Ava has the scarf draped around Mimi's neck, measuring the end with a floppy ruler and writing numbers down on a pad of paper.

"I would assume so," Aunt Rebecca answers. "And I guess these two will be each other's maids of honor someday, huh?" She gestures between Ava and me. "They're as good as sisters."

"Right," Mom says. "Those will be some fun times. But don't get any bright ideas, girls. We don't need any weddings around here for another twenty years or so."

"Twenty! I'll be almost thirty-three by then," I protest.

"Mmm, you're right," Mom says. "Twenty-five years, then."

I roll my eyes and then look over at Ava for support, but she's facing down, silently counting stitches along the scarf, and ignoring all of us. I join Mom at the kitchen table and decide to sit silently until I am spoken to. That will show Ava that two can play her little silent-treatment game. After all, I've had about as much silent-treatment over the past two days as one person can take.

The adults continue to drone on about the upcoming wedding, and Ava keeps fiddling with Mimi's scarf. Since no one is paying attention to me anyway, I pull my phone out of my pocket and open MM's website. I tap on the banner about the contest again and reread all of the rules and instructions. I can't wait to get home and finalize my sketches. I'd like to submit mine by the end of the day tomorrow at the very latest.

I close the site and type out a text to Bree: **Now my cousin's not speaking to me either. What is with this week?**

Maybe Mercury is in retrograde, Bree writes back.

What does that mean?

I don't know, but it's a thing, Bree replies. **What did you do to Ava?**

That's the problem—I don't even know, I tell her. **That's what makes it so weird.**

She and Deirdre should be friends, Bree answers, which makes me smile.

"What's so funny over there?" Mimi asks, and I snap my head up from my phone.

"Nothing," I answer. "Are you almost finished? I have homework to do." Mom looks at me curiously out of the corner of her eye.

"Am I, Ava?" Mimi asks.

"Yep," Ava says. "I'm going to have to put some finishing touches on, but I should have it complete later this week."

"We'll come by your house and drop it off, along with the jacket," Aunt Rebecca says, and I stand up from the table, hoping that will signal Mom and Mimi that we should leave now.

I say good-bye to Aunt Rebecca and Uncle Peter and kiss them on the cheeks. Then I walk over to Ava.

"Bye," I say, holding my hand out to do our wiggly finger salute.

"Bye," Ava says, placing her right cheek on mine and giving me an air kiss, keeping her hands wrapped up in the scarf the whole time. She turns away, heads down the hallway and back up the stairs, and disappears before I am even out the door.

Later that afternoon, when my dangly nameplate earring sketches are as perfect as I think I can make them, I leave my room and head up two flights of stairs to Mimi's. It's still odd for me to see all of her stuff crammed inside these four walls. As much as I love Blingingham Palace, this was the room I lived in since the first day I came home from the hospital. It still feels like mine somehow, even if I am glad that Mimi can call it home.

I tap my knuckles against the door gently, the rings on my hand brushing against the frame. This may be the first time I've ever knocked on this door, which is a strange feeling. I see Mimi perched on her vanity bench, rubbing moisturizer onto her forehead and cheeks. She turns at the sound of my tap. "Oh, Tessie," she says. "Come in, of course." I walk in and sit on top of the blanket chest, which is at the foot of Mimi's bed. As much as this room still feels like mine sometimes, it now has Mimi written all over it. What was once my stuffed (if completely organized) closet is now a mishmash of the wild patterns of Mimi's wardrobe. Her vanity overflows with makeup, and the entire surface of her dresser is covered with beads and gemstones and chains and all sorts of other jewels. I happen to know that two drawers of the dresser are jammed full of even more accessories, and that she keeps her most expensive pieces wrapped up in handkerchiefs on the highest shelf of the closet, or stuffed in old stockings under her mattress, or covered with tissues in the toes of her rain boots. Mimi's things are everywhere, and the scent of her perfume, while faint anytime she enters a room, is overwhelming in here. I breathe in deeply, finding it comforting.

"What's that you have there?" Mimi's back is to me, because she's still facing the mirror, but her eyes in the reflection are focused on mine.

"I wanted to show you my sketches," I tell her.

"Wonderful," Mimi says. "Let me see." I hold out the papers for Mimi to examine.

"Tell me which design you like best," I request.

"Oh, these are so fun," Mimi says. "What are you going to do with these?"

"They're for that contest. Re—" I stop myself from asking "Remember?" She doesn't. Not right now anyway.

"A fashion site I like is having a contest for who can design the best new accessory," I explain again. "This is my idea."

"I love them," Mimi says. "You should definitely win."

"Which is your favorite?"

"Hmm." Mimi considers each very carefully, nodding to herself while studying them. "I like them all, but I think this one is especially great." The sketch she's chosen features a small studded ball holding the earring in the earlobe, with each letter of the name dangling on top of one another underneath, connected by miniature versions of the same type of ball.

"Good, I like that one too," I tell her. "Thanks for your

84

help. And for this." I place the heart of the locket in my hand and squeeze it. "Can I ask you a question about it?"

"Of course," Mimi says.

"Why did you give it to me?" I ask. "Why not Ava, or Hayden, or Harper? They're all older than me."

"You are my only daughter's daughter," Mimi tells me seriously. "That gives you a very special position. But more important . . ." She trails off, and I can't tell if she's pausing for suspense or if she forgot what she was about to say.

"Yes?" I prompt her. "But more important . . . what?"

"You're my favorite," she finishes. "Of course you are."

Chapter 11

I hold off on submitting my contest entry online until the next day, reexamining the sheet over and over before I do. Every time I think I may be finished, I end up adding some extra details, until I finally feel ready to scan the paper, upload it onto Miscellaneous Moxie's contest site, and press Submit.

When I stand up from my desk chair, my right foot has fallen asleep and the muscles between my shoulder blades are stiff from being hunched over for hours. I hobble around Blingingham Palace to pull my phone out of the cushions of my couch, which is where I hide it when I don't want to be distracted. I close my eyes before looking at the screen, secretly hoping to see a text from Deirdre or Ava. When I glance down, I see a whole stream of messages waiting for me.

All of them from Bree.

I scan them quickly, but she is mostly babbling on about her audition tomorrow. I stuff my phone back into the couch without answering and head upstairs to my family, trying to keep the anticipation of hearing back from MM, along with all of my other worries, pushed out of my mind until tomorrow.

When I arrive at our usual corner on Monday morning, I find Bree and her trusty flute waiting for me, but there is no sign of Deirdre. "This is getting ridiculous," I say to Bree in greeting. "How long can this go on?"

"Hey, it's more important than ever that I bond with this thing—Frida, I've named her—because if I even have a chance of whooping those eighth graders' butts, I really need to—"

"I was talking about Deirdre." I interrupt Bree's rambling. "How can she still not be talking to us?"

"Who said I'm not talking?" I hear a voice behind me, and I whip around to find Deirdre standing with one hand on her hip, glirking at me with amusement in her eyes.

"Um, you," I point out. "You're the one who's been silent for three days straight."

"I had a gymnastics meet," Deirdre says. "And plus, you two were annoying."

"So we're not annoying anymore?" Bree asks.

"Well, now it's time to pay your penance," Deirdre says. "You say you don't know Rocco. Fine. After today you will. He's going to eat lunch with us."

"Today? Does it have to be today?" Bree asks. I shoot her a look out of the corner of my eye—we just got Deirdre back, and Bree already seems ready to make her mad again.

"It's not that he can never eat lunch with us," Bree continues. "It's just that, you know, the three of us have kind of a routine. And I really need to concentrate on my audition later, so I'd rather not have any of my routines disrupted today. So can't Rocco eat lunch with us tomorrow instead, so we can talk just the three of us today?"

"I can't disinvite him," Deirdre says matter-of-factly.

"Maybe we could reschedule for tomorrow?" I ask. "Tell him something came up."

"I'm not doing that," Deirdre says. "I'm eating lunch with Rocco today—you two can join us or not." She shifts her bag onto her other shoulder and heads down the hall toward our set of lockers, leaving Bree and me behind.

"What do we do now?" I turn to ask her, but Bree is kneeling on the floor of the hallway, her flute case open, with the largest middle piece in her hands. She looks under each key pad carefully, as if searching for a hidden treasure. "*Now* what are you doing?"

"I forgot to do the dried-spit check this morning," she

explains. "If there's any caught under Frida's pads, the keys will be sticky."

"Ew. Never mind. I don't really need the full explanation."

"Well, you asked," Bree says. "Thanks for answering my texts yesterday, by the way. Rude."

"I thought I did answer," I tell her. "Well, if I didn't, I meant to answer."

"Yeah, you didn't," Bree says. "At least Frida was there to calm me down about the audition."

"Okay, you really can't call that thing by a name," I tell her. "You sound like a legitimate crazy person."

"Shh, don't let Frida hear you talk that way!" Bree says, and I search her face for some clue that she's kidding, but she looks completely serious.

Scary serious.

"I'll let you two get back to bonding, then," I say. Then I turn down the hall and make my way toward our lockers, waiting for Bree to come to her senses and join me. But she hangs back with her new best friend, Frida, and by the time I reach my locker, Deirdre is nowhere in sight.

We aren't even in homeroom yet, and already the happy anticipation that the Miscellaneous Moxie contest gave me over the weekend seems a lifetime away.

For the first time that I can remember, I walk into the cafeteria alone, a firm sense of dread in the pit of my stomach. Bree is spending the lunch period in a band practice room, insisting that she needs the time to run through her scales in order to warm up her fingers. I look across the room to our usual spot, and I see Deirdre's profile on the bench.

With a boy's profile—Rocco's—in the place next to her. My place.

I take a deep breath to calm myself. *Be mature, be mature, be mature,* I recite in my head as I begin to make my way across the room. *It's only for one period,* I think. *Just be nice, so that Deirdre goes back to acting normal.*

When I am barely halfway to our table, my thoughts are interrupted as a girl I've never seen before appears in front of me, so abruptly that I almost walk right into her.

"Whoa, sorry," I say, moving to the side to try to step around her.

"It's Tess, right?" the girl asks me. I look more closely at her face, trying to place it in my memory, but nothing about it looks familiar.

"Yes?" I answer, confused.

"Can you tell me where you got your bracelet?" the girl asks, pointing to my right wrist, where my watch, bangle, and beads stand stacked on top of one another. "Actually, all of your bracelets. I love all of them."

"Oh, these?" I ask, still flustered. "Um, most of them

came from Threads—you know, the store on Twining Ridge Road?"

The girl nods. "I've been there," she says. "But I never know what to get." She waves her hand to people behind my back, gesturing for them to approach us. In seconds, three more girls have gathered around me, none of whom look any more familiar than the first one.

"Tess said the bracelets came from Threads," this girl tells the others, and I feel all eight of their eyes on me, looking me up and down, like I'm a mannequin in a store window.

Which is kind of a strange feeling, honestly.

"Sorry," I begin tentatively, not wanting to sound impolite, "but how do you know me?"

"We don't," one of the other girls pipes up. "But you have the best clothes. No, not clothes— I mean, your clothes are good too. But you make them look amazing with all of your . . . bling and stuff."

"Really?" I say. "Thanks. That's . . . that's really nice, but, like, how do— What grade are you in?"

"Sixth," two of them answer at once. "You're like our fashion icon."

I laugh out loud at this, believing she's kidding, but she looks just as serious as Bree did about giving her flute a name. "That's really flattering," I tell them. "But really, I think you're giving me too much credit."

"We're not," the first girl speaks for all of them. "We try to spot you in the hallways every single day, just to see what kind of outfit you've put together. Especially your accessories."

"Which I know sounds creepy, like we're stalking you or something," her friend adds. "But I promise we're not."

"I've been wanting to ask you about your bracelets for weeks," the first girl tells me. "But you're always with your friends, and I didn't want to interrupt, because, you know, lowly sixth grader and all."

"No, no, don't think like that," I tell them. "Trust me, I'm not cool. You could always just ask me whatever you want."

"Really? Because we have a lot of questions, actually," one of the other girls states. "I mean, if we could pick your brain for a while, we could really use some help."

"Our first dance of the year is on Friday, and we have no clue what we're supposed to wear," another says. "Maybe you could give us some ideas."

"I mean, I'd be happy to, but I'm not sure how much help I can be," I say, glancing at Deirdre's profile again. She's speaking to Rocco, her back facing the rest of the room. "Do you want to talk now?"

"Really? Don't you have to go to your friends?" the first girl asks.

"They're . . . otherwise occupied today," I say. "It's no problem. You'd actually be doing me a favor." The sixth graders lead me to their table, and the second we're seated, they launch in with a thousand questions about both my wardrobe and their own. The lunch period flies by so quickly with all of their chatter that we don't even get a chance to talk about their upcoming dance.

"Do you think we could do this again?" the first girl (whose name, I have learned, is Gianna) asks.

"Sure, this was fun," I tell them. "And actually, if you want, I can give you my number, and you can text me if you have any questions when we're not in school. Or find me on ExtraUniverse—Tess Maven."

"Awesome." The girls punch my number into their phones, and we then leave the cafeteria in opposite directions. I walk down the hall to Ms. Castleby's class, eager to get there early so I can ask her a question of my own, one about my business plan project.

Because sometimes, I think, it takes some new friends to give you your greatest ideas.

Chapter 12

I don't see one journal in Ms. Castleby's classroom, and I take that as a good sign that she didn't finish reading them yet. After all, she would have to be some kind of magician if she could read five classes' worth of journals over one weekend, right? She probably didn't even get to mine, so I still have a couple more days to come up with a good explanation for why Kayte's and my entries look so similar.

"Tess," she greets me as I approach her desk, the rest of the room still empty. "How are you? I'm sorry to say I didn't get to your journal yet. I'm hoping to have them all back by the end of the week. I really do look forward to reading yours."

I smile at Ms. Castleby, feeling sheepish, but no sense in raising the red flag on the journal situation now.

Maybe she won't even notice how much Kayte's and mine resemble each other. Or maybe she'll know automatically that Kayte must have copied me somehow. It's not like I've ever given Ms. Castleby a reason to think I would steal someone else's idea. "Can I ask you a quick question about the business plan project?" I ask her. "I thought I had come up with an idea over the weekend, but now I have a different one, and I think I may like it better."

"Of course," Ms. Castleby says as the first of my classmates begins to trickle into the room. "Is it quick? Because we'll have to start soon." She points to the classroom clock.

"It's quick," I promise. "So I was initially thinking of creating an accessory business where I designed new accessories. But then I couldn't figure out how that would work exactly, because I don't know how to actually make things—I just know how to sketch them on paper. And I'm not really that great at drawing, either, so it usually takes me, like, thirty sheets of paper to get one design right, which seems like a waste of time, if you're running a business and all." Half of my class is now inside and taking their seats, so I really have to get to the point soon if I'm going to get Ms. Castleby's opinion.

"So I was thinking instead . . . ," I continue. "What if I give advice on accessorizing? Like how to put things together, what to pair with a particular outfit, help picking out new items to purchase, that kind of stuff."

"Intriguing," Ms. Castleby says. "I think you definitely have the start of a great idea there. Why don't you try to flesh it out more tonight, so that you can discuss it with your classmates tomorrow and see what they think?"

"I will." I nod, and I thank Ms. Castleby before taking my seat. I kind of wanted her to tell me that this was the best idea she had ever heard, and while she didn't say it was terrible, she didn't seem to love it either. Maybe I just need to come up with a better way of explaining it. Maybe I need to get my ideas down on paper, and then I'll understand the concept better myself.

Or maybe it's just a lousy idea.

"Real nice." Deirdre's voice pulls me out of mulling over my business plan. "I had a great lunch. Thanks for joining us." She slides into her chair and keeps her back toward me, and a familiar pit forms in my stomach. I hate when we're in an argument, but I especially hate when we're in an argument and I know it's my fault.

This is my fault.

I didn't even try to talk to Deirdre and Rocco at lunch. I ignored that side of the cafeteria completely after my sixth-grade "fans" appeared. Of course, I had intended to go sit with Deirdre. That was where I was heading when Gianna came up to me.

96

But Deirdre doesn't know that. Deirdre just thinks I refused to sit with her and Rocco.

I look across the room to Bree for a show of support. Is this the time of her audition? Shouldn't I know what time that is? She has only been talking about it for weeks, and I didn't even wish her good luck, after completely forgetting to text her back yesterday.

Now not only am I not being a conscientious student, but I'm not even being a conscientious friend. Or at least not a thoughtful one.

"Hey." I tap Deirdre on the shoulder with the tip of my orange gel pen—my least favorite color, for Monday. "I'm sorry I didn't sit with you at lunch today. Something came up. Really." Deirdre shrugs her shoulders without turning around as Ms. Castleby begins class. I run my fingers through my hair, thinking about what I can do to solve all of the problems that seem to keep springing up. I feel as though I can't even try to come up with a solution for one before another appears.

The missing ring.

Kayte's identical journal.

Deirdre's anger.

Ava's annoyance.

Bree's disappointment.

Not to mention all of my schoolwork, particularly the business plan. If I don't start getting at least some of these problems solved one by one, I fear they'll begin exploding all around me.

I think about what I can do immediately to start fixing things, and I pull my phone out of my bag silently. Hiding the glow of the screen under my left hand, I quickly type a message to Bree with my right thumb. **Break a leg. You're amazing. xo**

I stuff my phone back into my bag and return my attention to Ms. Castleby.

"Pick a partner or two to bounce ideas off of for a few minutes, before your larger group discussion tomorrow," she announces, and then she looks at me. "I've heard from a couple of people that you already have ideas that you're looking for help fleshing out, so I thought I'd give you the chance to get a little head start today. Get into groups of two or three and choose an area of the classroom to work in. I'll give you fifteen minutes to talk."

I tap Deirdre again on the back with my pen. "Partners?" I ask.

Deirdre turns around to face me, and I gather my notebook to move to the chair next to her. But then I realize that Deirdre isn't looking at me at all—she's looking past me over my shoulder, and she then nods her head enthusiastically.

"I'm working with Rocco," she tells me coldly.

"Do you want to join us, Tess?" he asks. "Ms. Castleby said we could have three." I glance back at Deirdre for her approval, but she is merely moving to the seat next to Rocco, ignoring both of us.

"That would be great, thanks," I tell Rocco. I flip my chair around. "Listen, I'm really sorry I missed lunch with you guys." I face Rocco as I say this, since Deirdre won't look at me anyway. "All of these sixth graders kind of surrounded me, and I got distracted, but I hope you weren't offended."

"Not at all," Rocco says, and I smile at him gratefully. If he's not holding a grudge, then Deirdre shouldn't either, right? "What did the sixth-grade wolf pack want from you?"

I laugh at this, surprised that Rocco can actually make me laugh. Maybe Deirdre is right about him— maybe he is funny, and he is certainly nice enough. It's slowly starting to make more sense how these two could have struck up a real friendship.

"Well, funny you should ask," I begin. "Because what they were talking about kind of inspired a new business plan idea. I'd really like to hear what you think, if you don't mind me starting."

"Let's hear it," Rocco says, leaning forward on his

desk. I glance at Deirdre, silently asking permission, and she nods, giving me a small grin. In that second I feel like my best friend is back, finally looking again like the Deirdre I know.

Hopefully, that's one problem on its way to being solved, at least temporarily.

Chapter 13

Deirdre and Rocco both listen intently as I explain the bare bones of my business idea, and once I finish, Rocco announces, "So you'd be a consultant."

"Right," Deirdre agrees with him. "An accessorizing consultant. I think it's brilliant."

"Really?" I ask. "Do you think that's something people would pay for? I mean, it sounds a little formal—'consultant.'"

"Then call yourself a stylist," Deirdre says instantly. "That sounds much more Hollywood."

"Accessory stylist," Rocco brainstorms. "The accessory stylist of Twining Ridge Middle School?"

"Nah, that doesn't have much ring to it," Deirdre disagrees. "What's that word you've been using? Oh, 'bling.' Bling stylist. *That* sounds like something interesting."

"Am I supposed to know what bling is?" Rocco asks.

"Don't worry about it," Deirdre tells him. "It's a girl thing." She turns back to me. "So prices—what will you charge?"

"I have no idea," I say. "Maybe, like, fifty cents for a consultation, and—"

"Fifty cents? Are you crazy?" Deirdre cuts me off. "You need to charge more than that."

"I agree," Rocco says. "The more you charge, the more exclusive people will think your business is."

"But I can't be too expensive," I argue. "Or else no one will be able to pay at all."

"Okay, let's map this out," Rocco says, tearing a sheet of paper out of his binder. "What are the services you'll be providing? Consultation is one, which is really just giving them advice in a conversation, right? Do you want to charge by the minute, like a lawyer charges by the hour?"

"Um, I think that's a little intense," I say. "How about I just make it a standard fifteen-minute advice-giving session?"

"Good," Rocco says, writing that on his paper. "Three dollars. What else?"

"Don't you think that's a little high?" I ask.

"It might be," Rocco says, "but that's not where you want to make a lot of your money. You make the simplest-sounding service the most expensive so that people will want to pay for a package. So if three dollars buys a fifteen-minute chat, but for five dollars they can get the chat *and* something else, they'll think that's a bargain, and you make more money."

I look at Deirdre with wide eyes, impressed. "Yeah, he's brilliant," she says. "Trust me, I know. He helped me map out my whole business plan this weekend." I want to ask when this happened, since Deirdre claimed to have been at a gymnastics meet all weekend, but there is no way I want to strike up another war between us, so I let it go.

"What is your plan?" I ask her. "We haven't even talked about either of yours yet."

"Mine is tumbling lessons. His is tutoring," Deirdre says quickly. "But back to you—yours is much more interesting, and plus, ours are pretty much done already. So for five dollars, how about if you give them advice and let them borrow some piece of yours? She has an accessory collection like you would not believe." She says this last part to Rocco.

"And if they lose that accessory, or stain it or whatever, they have to pay double—so instead of five dollars, they then owe you ten," Rocco adds.

"So you shouldn't lend out anything worth too much, in case you need to replace it," Deirdre reasons.

"And then you should have one 'premiere package' or something—like you take them out shopping one-on-one to help them choose accessories of their own, or you do the shopping for them. For ten dollars—maybe fifteen—plus the cost of the item," Rocco states, jotting this down on his paper. "Here." He hands the sheet to me. "What do you think?"

I read over Rocco's notes and nod my head.

"So I know Ms. Castleby said we don't actually have to put our plan into practice," I begin, "but I think I might try to. I mean, those sixth graders wanted fashion advice for their dance on Friday. Do you think it would be mean if I used them as my guinea pigs, to see if they'd go for the idea?"

"Absolutely use them," Deirdre says. "You can't be working for free. Plus, they probably have friends—better to lay the groundwork for your future early."

I tilt my head and stare at her. "Since when do you use the term 'lay the groundwork'?" I ask. "You sound like a forty-seven-year-old accountant."

Deirdre points to Rocco, who smiles innocently.

"Okay, wrap up what you're discussing," Ms. Castleby calls. "We need to move on for now." Just then Bree walks through the classroom door, her flute missing from her arms for the first time in days. She crosses the room to her desk without stopping.

"Thank you for your help," I say to Deirdre and Rocco as I flip my chair back around. "You two are lifesavers."

"Anytime," Rocco says. "I like this stuff."

"Yeah, he likes it a little too much," Deirdre teases him as she slides into her own seat. I look across the room and finally catch Bree's eye.

"How'd it go?" I mouth to her.

Bree just shakes her head and then turns to face the front of the room. I try to get her attention to ask if she wants to meet in the bathroom, but she won't look in my direction. Maybe now she's the one who's mad at me. It certainly wouldn't be the first time this week that I'm on someone's silent-treatment list.

Even though I know it could get me in trouble, I pull my phone out of my bag, risking the consequences. I type a fast text to Bree. **Do you want to meet in the bathroom and talk?**

I look across the room and see her peer down at her lap, where her phone is resting, hidden from Ms. Castleby's view.

Nope, she writes back.

Talk later? I ask.

Not about this, she says curtly.

I send her a sad face.

It's just one audition, Bree writes. I'll get over it.

I'm sure you were great, I say.

I wasn't, Bree says. But I really don't want to talk about it.

Got it. But we're okay, right? I ask.

Why wouldn't we be?

My good luck text was late, I respond. And I didn't text you back yesterday. Sorry about both.

No worries, Bree writes back. Is Deirdre mad about lunch?

I think that's okay now, I say. I hope. But if you apologize too, that probably wouldn't hurt.

Fine, will do, Bree says.

I return my phone to my bag with a relieved sigh, thankful that, at least for now, the three of us are back to normal once again.

I explain my new business plan idea to Mimi as we walk together to meet Toby at his bus. "Do you think people would actually pay for that?" I ask. "Deirdre and Rocco said yes, but I don't know. Is it too expensive?"

"If it is, the customers will let you know right away," Mimi says. "By not paying for it. That's how we used to know if we had overpriced a piece in the shop." Until last year, Mimi sold antiques in a small store on Twining Ridge Road. She loved it there—loved the antiques and

106

loved interacting with the customers. But slowly there started to be problems. She would charge the wrong price for an item, or she would sell a piece that a customer had already placed on hold, or she wouldn't lock the door before leaving the shop if she was the one closing up. Mimi hasn't talked much about working at the store since she had to leave, so I think it's a good sign that she has brought it up now.

"So what would you do then?" I ask. "If there was something in the store that wasn't selling?"

"Well, it depended on the piece," Mimi says. "If customers seemed interested in it until they saw the price tag—and this happened a significant amount of times—then we usually dropped the price, and that tended to do the trick."

"So if no one will pay the three, five, or ten dollars for the services I'm offering, then I know that they're too expensive," I say.

"Exactly," Mimi agrees. "Then, of course, some items in the store just wouldn't sell no matter how inexpensive they were. They say one person's trash is another person's treasure, but in some cases, it's really just trash." I laugh at this, but Mimi's statement also makes me nervous. This whole "bling stylist" idea might just be a bad one, no matter what the prices are. Is it even worth trying at all? Because what if it's a big fat flop?

"Do you think I should do it?" I ask Mimi as we reach the bus stop corner. "Or do you think I should scrap the whole thing? I mean, I could still do it for my language arts project, but should I try to put it into practice?"

"I absolutely think you should," Mimi tells me. "If you don't try, how will you ever know?" The headlights of Toby's bus appear down the street, and Mimi and I stand lost in our own thoughts until it pulls up in front of us and Toby steps off.

"Carl, there you are," Mimi calls when she sees him. "Let me zip that jacket for you."

"Carl?" Toby asks as he approaches. "That's Uncle Carl's name."

I feel my own cheeks flush at Mimi's mistake, and the last thing I want Toby to do is harp on it and make her feel bad. "Let's go, you," I call to him, but Toby won't take the hint.

"Mimi, why did you call me Carl?"

"Just a slip of the tongue, my boy," Mimi tells him. I glance at her briefly, and she looks just like the Mimi I've known my whole life—the rosy cheeks, thick dark eyelashes, perfect lipstick, dangly earrings. But a flash of something different darts across her eyes, so fast that I almost miss it. It's a look of blankness, and it worries me more than anything else that has happened this week.

"You didn't bring my scooter?" Toby interrupts my thoughts, but at least he's dropped the name problem.

"You can use your own legs to walk home for once," I say. "Last one there is a rotten egg." Toby sprints off down the sidewalk, his book bag flapping against his back like a heavy cape. Mimi and I begin to follow him.

"So at the store, which was the hardest piece you ever had to sell?" I ask her. "The one thing that no one ever wanted?"

Mimi takes a few steps silently, and I assume she is thinking about the answer. When she still says nothing, I prod, "Mimi?"

"Yes, Tessie?"

"Which was the hardest piece you ever had to try to sell?"

"Sell where?" Mimi asks.

"At the—" I cut myself off. If she's having a bad memory episode, I should just accept it. I shouldn't upset her more with questions she can't remember the answers to right now.

"I won!" Toby calls from the bottom of our driveway, and I give him a thumbs-up. Mimi and I walk the rest of the way home quietly, each feeling lost, but in different ways.

Chapter 14

I leave Mimi and Toby alone in the kitchen and take my bag downstairs to my room. When I pull out my phone, a huge stream of waiting text messages greets me. Every single one of them is from a number I don't know, from someone whose contact information isn't stored in my phone. I scroll down to the first one and open it.

Hey, it's Gianna. Thanks again for today. Can I send you some pictures of the outfits I'm thinking of for Friday?

The next: Hi, Tess, this is Ellie. We talked at lunch. Would you put a necklace on top of a turtleneck, or skip it? Thank you for your help!

And then: Hello. You don't know me, but I got your number from Gianna. Do you know where I could get a chain with one of those evil eye charms hanging from the middle? I'm pretty sure I've seen you with one. I'm hoping to get it before Friday's dance.

Overwhelmed, I scroll back to Gianna's text and write, **Hey, thanks for your message. So if you and your friends are interested, I run an accessory styling business, and I'd be happy to work with you guys. It's called . . .**

I think for a moment. I need a name that will make my business sound legitimate, where it won't just seem like I thought of it off the top of my head. I look around my room, and my eyes settle on Blingingham Palace.

The Bling Queen, I type. **Fifteen-minute advice sessions for $3, advice plus an accessory loan for $5, and a shopping trip for $10. Can you spread the word to your friends, and anyone who wants to can meet me at my locker tomorrow morning before school?**

I press Send and then wait. This could be the end of my business before it even begins. If Gianna thinks this is a waste of her money, then her friends will almost certainly think the same. My entire enterprise rests in the hands of a sixth grader who I didn't even know a few hours ago.

My phone buzzes with a new text, and I read, **Sounds great! I'll let everyone know. See you tomorrow!** I smile widely to myself as I add Gianna to my contacts. I toss my phone onto the couch cushions and stand up. Then I twirl around the middle of Blingingham Palace to my own victory dance, no musical accompaniment needed.

A whole gaggle of sixth-grade girls greets me at my locker the next morning—Gianna and her three friends from yesterday's lunch, plus a couple of new girls who I've never seen before. They wave enthusiastically when I walk through the door at the end of the hallway.

"None of us knew exactly which one your locker was," Gianna says as I approach. "We had to ask someone."

"Oh, sorry," I say. "I should have told you."

"No problem," Gianna says. "So I told everyone here about your business, and we're ready to sign up. Do you think you could fit all of us in before Friday's dance?"

"Wow, um, I'll certainly try," I tell them. "I mean, yes. Yes, I will." That's the first step of running a good business, I think—sounding confident. "What is usually easiest"—I say "usually" as if I have done this for years—"is if everyone texts me what they're looking for. Then I'll schedule some time for us to meet, or I'll pull some lending options from my collection, or we'll set a date to go shopping. I can also go shopping for you, if that's easier and if that's what you prefer."

"And when do we pay you?" the girl who I remember as Ellie asks.

"Up front," I answer definitively. "Oh, and as insurance, anyone who borrows anything from my personal collection, if it's lost or damaged or anything like that, I charge an additional five dollars." The girls all nod like this makes complete sense, and I am impressed with myself at how official I sound. "Does everyone have my number? Once you do, text me your name, request, and timeline—when you would need to have this done by—and I'll get back to you after school, once I can put together a schedule."

"I'll send your number to anyone who doesn't have it," Gianna says. "This is awesome."

"Great. Thanks so much, guys," I say. "I look forward to hearing from you." I'm pretty sure I sound like a real business owner now.

The sixth graders turn and retreat down the hallway, calling excited good-byes over their shoulders. And when they have scattered, I see who has been standing at the back of their pack, listening the entire time.

Kayte.

"Snooping much?" I ask her.

"They asked me where your locker was," Kayte answers. "I didn't request to be involved in your little enterprise."

"You could have left at any time," I say, moving toward my locker and then twirling out the combination.

"You know what you're doing is illegal, right?" Kayte asks.

"Excuse me?"

"You can't exchange money on school property," Kayte tells me. "Not for services rendered. It's in the school manual."

She read the school manual?

"I wasn't exchanging money," I say. "And services certainly weren't being rendered, whatever that means."

"It didn't sound that way to me," Kayte says. "I would shut down this little mooching operation right now before someone reports you for stealing from the poor, innocent sixth graders."

"That's not what I'm doing, and you also can't threaten me, you know," I say. "I'm sure 'Don't threaten your classmates' is also in the manual."

"Wait until Ms. Castleby hears about this," Kayte says. "First you're a copycat, and now you're a thief."

"Ms. Castleby is the one who gave me the entire idea," I say. "I mean, her project did. I'm sure she'll be happy to hear I'm actually putting it into practice."

"Do you want to test that theory right now?" Kayte asks. "There she is." Kayte takes off down the hall toward Ms. Castleby's classroom before I can answer her, and I hurry to catch up. Ms. Castleby is still unlocking her door when Kayte reaches her.

"Ms. Castleby?" she asks in what I know Kayte thinks is her sweet voice. "Can I ask you a question?"

"Of course," Ms. Castleby answers. "Come in while I get settled." I trail Kayte into the classroom.

"Ms. Castleby, about the business plan project—" I begin, trying to get out ahead of Kayte, but Ms. Castleby cuts me off.

"Sorry, Tess. Kayte was here first," she says, and Kayte smirks at me with a gloating look on her face.

"I heard one of my classmates is planning to put her business into practice here at school," Kayte says. "But isn't it against the rules to buy and sell things on school grounds?"

"The 'classmate' she's talking about is me," I interrupt before Ms. Castleby can answer. "I've started an accessory consultancy business." I use Rocco's phrasing to make me sound more official. "But I'm not exchanging any money at school. It's all being done on our own time, away from here."

"I don't see any issues, then," Ms. Castleby says. "If the money isn't being exchanged on school property, it's fine. Is there anything else?" Ms. Castleby looks back and forth between Kayte and me.

"But I thought we weren't supposed to actually set up the businesses," Kayte protests.

"You certainly don't have to as part of your assignment

grade," Ms. Castleby tells her. "But I think it shows a lot of initiative if you do. In fact, Tess, once I hear more about what your business entails, I may have to be your first customer."

I grin widely at Ms. Castleby, silently thanking her. "I would be honored. But you may have to get in line," I tell her. "There's a whole slew of sixth graders I'm currently dealing with."

Kayte turns on her heel and leaves the classroom, murmuring "Thanks for nothing" under her breath. I say good-bye to Ms. Castleby and call "thank you" over my shoulder as I follow Kayte into the hallway.

"So there," I say as I pass her, trotting down the hall to where I see Deirdre and Bree at their lockers. As soon as they spot me, they head in my direction. I call out, "You're never going to believe what just happened."

"Ooh, tell us," Deirdre says.

"Yeah, I could use some good news right now," Bree agrees. They come on either side of me and link their arms through mine, and I begin to recount the story.

And as much as they could drive me crazy, I had to admit that they were the two best accessories I could ever find.

That is, when we were speaking to each other.

Chapter 15

That night I create a spreadsheet on my computer for the Bling Queen orders that have been texted to me since this morning. I've already received six orders: two for fifteen-minute styling consultations, and four more requests to borrow a piece of mine. I decide that the easiest way to do this will be to have everyone over to Blingingham Palace at once, especially since we don't have much time left before Friday's dance. After I get permission from my parents (assuring them that this actually *is* for school, since it's related to Ms. Castleby's business plan project), I reply to each girl individually, asking if she can stop by between four and five thirty p.m. tomorrow. As the "yes" texts begin pouring in, I tap out a message to Deirdre and Bree.

Want to come over to my place tomorrow? I'm doing

my first Bling Queen event from 4:00 to 5:30. Kind of like an open house.

I'll be there, Bree writes back instantly. And a few minutes later Deirdre replies, **Me too.** I begin outlining my pitch for Friday's business plan speech, feeling pretty good that this project, and the business itself, just may turn out to be less of a failure than I had feared.

A note from Ms. Castleby is waiting on my desk in homeroom the next morning, asking me to come see her as soon as I get in. I show it to my homeroom teacher and then dart out the door toward her classroom, pulling my phone out of my pocket so I'm prepared to write down whatever she has chosen as her first Bling Queen order. After all, I can't very well ask Ms. Castleby to text me, right? That would be weird.

I breeze into her room and then come to a sudden halt. Because standing on the other side of Ms. Castleby's desk is none other than Kayte Reynolds.

And if there's anything I've learned lately, it's that no good ever comes from a Kayte Reynolds sighting.

"Oh good, you're both here," Ms. Castleby says. "So I was trying to finish up the journals last night, and I noticed something curious about the two of yours." I swear my stomach does a cartwheel then. I have been so busy getting Bling Queen up and going that I had all but forgotten about our nearly identical journals.

What is Ms. Castleby going to do to us? Report us to the principal for copying? Make us rewrite all of our entries? Can I ever get her to believe that I absolutely, positively did not copy Kayte? No matter what, I'm pretty sure I won't be receiving an A+ on this assignment.

"By any chance do you two read Miscellaneous Moxie?" Ms. Castleby asks, and I am instantly confused. What does MM have to do with anything? Shouldn't she be scolding us or something?

"Um, yes?" I answer, and I see Kayte nodding, looking just as confused as I feel.

"I could tell," Ms. Castleby continues. "I was trying to figure out what your journal writing reminds me of, and that's it—Miscellaneous Moxie's blog posts." Kayte and I stay quiet, waiting for the next part, where Ms. Castleby says we've been plagiarizing, or copying each other. I mean, I guess it makes sense that my journal has the same tone as MM's—I do read it more than anything else, and I write about the same stuff. But is that a bad thing?

"I mean that as a compliment," Ms. Castleby says when Kayte and I don't respond. "You each have a very distinct voice in your journal—different from each other's, and different from Miscellaneous Moxie's. But they are both strong. And the style is similar."

I glance at Kayte, but her face is still unreadable as she stares at Ms. Castleby.

"It was the way you decorated your entries that finally helped me figure it out—with the little illustrations and multicolored underlining and whatnot. That's exactly what Miscellaneous Moxie does, only with fonts and stuff. It makes for a great effect." Ms. Castleby finally seems finished.

"Oh, well, thank you," I answer when Kayte still doesn't say a word. "That's my favorite site."

"Yes, thank you," Kayte agrees, though she doesn't exactly sound like she means it.

"I secretly love that site too," Ms. Castleby says. "I may be too old for it, but oh well." She shrugs. "I was thinking, if you two ever have a project you want to try to do together, for extra credit or whatever, I think you could make quite the duo. What do you say?"

Kayte and I look at each other, and I can tell by the firm line her lips are making that she has no intention of agreeing to this.

"I'm actually having a Bling Queen—that's what I decided to name my business—open house at my place tonight," I volunteer. I mean, there is no way Kayte will ever go for this, but I'll at least look like I'm making the effort in front of Ms. Castleby.

"What time?" Kayte asks, back to her sweet voice, I'm sure for Ms. Castleby's benefit.

"Four to five thirty," I answer, and then I turn to Ms. Castleby. "You're welcome to come by too, if you want, but I'm also happy to pick something out for you, if you're interested."

"I am," Ms. Castleby says. "But I think I might prefer you choosing and buying an item for me. That's something you offer, right?"

"Of course," I tell her. "Just give me an idea of what you're looking for, and when you need it by, and I'll get right on it."

"How much is that again?" Ms. Castleby asks.

"Ten dollars," I answer. "Plus the cost of the item."

"Great," Ms. Castleby says. "I'll mail you the money, so we don't exchange it on school grounds. Will that work?" And I get the feeling that she is saying all of this in front of Kayte for a reason, as if she wants Kayte to know that we're not breaking any rules.

"Of course," I tell her. "So maybe I'll see you later." I say this last part to Kayte as I turn to leave the room, knowing for certain that there is no way I will.

"I'll be there," Kayte answers, and I turn around quickly with my eyebrows raised. What is she up to?

Is she just agreeing now because Ms. Castleby is listening?

"Do you need my address?" I ask her innocently.

"I remember it," she tells me.

"Okay, then," I say. "See you later." I rush off to my homeroom ahead of her, dying to tell Deirdre and Bree about what just happened. But if I tell them ahead of time, that might make things worse. I need to keep tonight professional—all Bling Queen, all the time. I can't have them picking a fight with Kayte, in case Kayte actually does show up.

I twirl the heart of my locket between my fingers again and again as our homeroom teacher takes attendance, and I decide to keep quiet about this development, at least for now.

The doorbell rings right at four p.m., and I rush up the stairs from where I was straightening Blingingham Palace. (To be fair, it's pretty neat at all times, but today I spread things out more and opened up my containers so the girls can examine things more easily.)

"I'll get it!" Toby rushes to the door just ahead of me and flings it open.

"Toby, no!" I try to stop him. No official business owner should have her little brother answering the door, but Toby is insistent. Gianna and two of her friends stand on our stoop, each clutching cash in her hand and looking excited.

My very first clients.

"Come in, come in." I open the door wider and pull Toby out of the way. "Toby, how about you go hang out with Mimi?"

"No, thank you," he answers, which makes the sixth graders laugh. Unfortunately, this only encourages Toby more.

"Do you want to see my room?" he asks them.

"No, they definitely do not," I say. "They're here for business. But I'll tell you what—the doorbell is going to ring a few more times, so if you want to be in charge of letting those people in, that can be your job. I'll stay in my room to work with these girls."

"Okay, I'll do it!" Toby says, and he sits on the bottom two steps with his chin in his hands, facing the front door and waiting. I lead the sixth graders toward the basement, and they follow me down the steps.

"Your room is in the basement?" one of them asks.

"Yeah," I say. "My grandmother moved in with us last summer, so she took my room, and my parents made me my own place in the basement. Here we are." I walk them past the bed and desk side of my space and straight into the middle of my fake closet. "I call it Blingingham Palace, which I know sounds kind of corny, but it helped me think of the Bling Queen name for the business."

The girls look around with wide eyes. "The shelves on this side are where I keep my accessories, so this is what we'll be focusing on," I continue, impressed again by how official I think I sound. "You can take a few minutes to look around. Then whoever is ready first can meet me on that couch under the window to start your consultation. Sound good?"

"Great!" they answer, and they begin moving along the wall of bookshelves, examining each nook and cranny. I settle myself on the couch and wait for one of them to join me.

"I have a question," Gianna begins. "You know that locket you were wearing earlier? Is it possible to borrow that?"

"No, sorry," I say, placing my hand over my empty chest, as if expecting it to be there. I took all of my accessories off before anyone arrived, and placed the loanable items on the shelves and the off-limits pieces next to my computer. "That was a gift from my grandmother, so I can't risk anything happening to it."

"Understood." Gianna nods.

"But I do have some other great long chains with charms hanging off them, if that's what you're looking for," I tell her, standing up and walking over to my necklace section. I hear footsteps on the stairs and look over the tops of the shelves to see Deirdre and Bree barreling down them. I wave hello and point them to my bed. "Do you guys want to sit there? Or you're welcome to join us on this side, if you want."

"We'll stay here," Bree says, flopping down on top of my comforter. Deirdre is poking at her phone, not paying attention, and she walks straight into the edge of my desk.

"Ouch. Where'd that come from?" she asks.

"How about if you stop texting for a second and maybe you won't trip over your own feet?" Bree answers her. I leave them on their own and disappear back behind the bookshelves, putting all of my attention on my customers, just as a good business owner should.

Chapter 16

A half hour later the first Bling Queen open house is going better than I ever could have imagined. After our talk, Gianna chose a rhinestone flower comb to place in her hair—we decided during her consultation that she should pull her hair into a ponytail in order to better show off the lacy detail on the shoulders of the shirt she picked to wear on Friday. Ellie decided on a pair of black suspenders decorated with bright pink hearts to wear with the simple turtleneck and flared skirt she plans on sporting. And Natasha went for a mood ring, which we agree will be an easy way of starting a conversation with someone at the dance.

I have each of the girls sign Bling Queen contracts, which I created and printed out before they arrived, specifying what they're borrowing and that they are aware they will owe me an additional five dollars if anything is lost, broken, or stained. I collect the cash they give me in a faux fur change purse, an item that I have been eager to use for years. Finally I have found the perfect reason—my very first non-allowance, non-gift money. Somehow earning it on my own makes the dollar bills look so much more special than when they are simply given to me in a birthday card.

I hear the doorbell ring again, and I wait for the sounds of footsteps on the stairs. Deirdre and Bree are both still sprawled out on my bed, each lost in the goings-on within her own phone, and I can barely hear over Gianna's, Ellie's, and Natasha's excited chatter. When a few more seconds go by and no additional customers appear, I yell Toby's name. Nothing.

"Excuse me one second, guys," I say, and I sprint up the stairs, ready to yell at Toby about not forcing any of my customers to take a tour of the LEGO sets in his room. But when I reach the foyer, Toby is nowhere to be found, and I fling the front door open myself.

Where I find Kayte and Ava waiting. Together.

Silently but together.

"Um, hi," I say. "You came?" This comes out as more of a question toward Kayte than I meant it to.

"I said I would," she answers without emotion.

"I'm here with Mimi's finished scarf, and the jacket from Mom," Ava pipes up. "Is Mimi here?"

"Yeah, of course," I tell her, opening the door wider for both of them to enter. "Are your parents with you?" I shut the door behind them.

"My dad's in the car, stuck on a conference call," Ava says. "You have people over?"

"Yes, I started a—" But I am interrupted by the sound of the doorbell again. "Sorry, just a second. Kayte, if you want to head downstairs, Ava can show you where the basement door is. And I think Mimi is in the living room." I open the front door and find three more sixth graders waiting. "Come in, come in," I greet them. "Gianna, Ellie, and Natasha are downstairs. They've already picked out their accessories."

I lead the new girls through the house and down the basement steps, where I find not only the five people I initially left down here, but also Kayte, Ava, and Toby.

"Toby, you're supposed to be manning the front door, remember?" I ask him, trying to shoo him back up the steps. But Toby is deep into a game of Thumb War with Ellie, and he shows no sign of listening anytime soon. Meanwhile, Kayte and Ava both stand in the center of the room, looking around with their mouths open.

"When did you move down here?" Ava asks.

"Right before Mimi moved in," I explain. "She took my room."

"It's— Wow," she says. "You're even more spoiled than I thought." She says this last part under her breath, but I hear it anyway. But I really don't have time to let Ava get to me right now, not when I have three more customers to attend to.

"Toby, move it or lose it," I say, taking him by the shoulders and hauling him to the other side of the room. "Here, girls." I gesture for the three new sixth graders to follow me. "Let me show you the ropes." I take them on a brief tour of Blingingham Palace, forcing myself to talk more and more loudly as the people around me become noisier and noisier. My new room feels huge when it's just me down here, but with all of these extra people, it is suddenly claustrophobic.

And deafening.

"Um, excuse me." I feel a tap on my shoulder, and I turn to find Deirdre facing me. "Why is Reynolds here?"

"It's a long story," I say. "But I really can't talk about it right now."

"You should have told me she was coming," Deirdre says. "I didn't come here to hang out with Kayte Reynolds."

"I didn't really have a choice," I try to explain. "Can we please just talk about this later? I have to take care of my customers."

Deirdre raises her eyebrows at this. "Well, you seem

very busy," she says, a biting tone in her voice. "I'll get out of your hair."

"No, Deirdre. I didn't mean—" I begin, but Deirdre raises her hand to stop me.

"It's fine," she says. "But I'm certainly not going to sit here with Kayte lurking around. I have things to do."

She marches out of Blingingham Palace and back to the other side of my room in a huff. I catch Bree's eye, hoping she'll do something to appease Deirdre, but she merely shrugs and turns back to her phone. I want to stop Deirdre, to put an end to this argument before it gets out of hand. But one of the sixth graders steps in front of me, grabbing my attention. And by the time I look toward the other side of the room again, Deirdre is gone.

I resolve to push that issue out of my mind for now, like any good business owner should, and concentrate on my customers instead. Even the girls who only planned to get a consultation end up borrowing a piece once they see my collection, so by the end of the open house, I've collected thirty dollars in my furry leopard change purse. Ava has already disappeared from the room, I'm guessing to go give Mimi her scarf and jacket, and Kayte left without saying good-bye (of course). I take the sixth graders back up the stairs and outside to their parents' waiting cars. I hug them each good-bye and thank them.

"Phew," I say to myself when I enter the house again,

and I walk into the kitchen to find Mimi at the table.

"Did Ava leave?" I ask her.

"She did," Mimi answers. "How did it go? You certainly seemed busy."

"It was great," I answer. "But Bree is still here. I have to go talk to her, since she came to be supportive."

"Of course," Mimi says. "Have fun." I trot downstairs and find Bree playing SLAP with Toby, his hands hovering over her palms as she sneakily tries to flip hers around and slap the tops of his. Toby is giggling loudly, and I begin to pull him by one foot off the bed.

"Let's go. I really have to talk to Bree now," I say. "Shoo, or else Tickle Claws is going to . . ." The tips of my fingers approach Toby's armpits, which is the only surefire way to get him to move quickly. He leaps off the bed with a squeal and runs upstairs, still giggling, and I collapse on top of my comforter.

"I'm exhausted," I say. "This running-a-business nonsense is harder than it looks."

"Yeah, I can tell," Bree says. "It was crazy in here."

"Thanks for coming," I tell her. "I appreciate it. Really."

"No worries," Bree says. "But just one question—"

"Why was Kayte Reynolds here, I know," I fill in for her. "It's a long story. I was kind of forced to ask her in front of Ms. Castleby today, but I never thought she'd actually show up."

"She was probably spying," Bree says. "So she can start copying your business idea, too, just like she copied your journal."

"I don't think she copied my journal, believe it or not," I tell Bree. "I think both of us may have been mimicking Miscellaneous Moxie's posts, without knowing the other one was doing it."

"But what are the chances that you both write about glitter on the same day?" Bree asks. "That's super-shady."

"Well, I mean, you saw Deirdre's belt . . . ," I begin. "It's possible that thing just caught both of our attentions, right?"

"I guess," Bree says. "I still think it's weird that she came."

"I do too," I say. "Hey, I know you don't really want to talk about it, but any word on first chair yet?"

"Nope. They're supposed to post it on Friday," Bree says. "I know I bombed the audition, though. I totally messed up the D-scale. They'll probably kick me out of band for being so terrible."

"You say that every time, and every time you're brilliant," I tell her.

"Not this time," Bree says. "Now are we going to discuss the real issue at hand?"

"Deirdre?" I ask.

"Bingo," Bree says. "I mean, trust me, it's not like I

was happy to see Kayte walk in, but I wasn't going to storm out over it. What did she say to you?"

"She was mad Kayte was here, and that I hadn't told her beforehand that Kayte would be coming," I say. "But I feel like there has to be more to the story. She was on her phone the whole time, and she rushed out claiming she had 'things to do.'"

"Do you think she was going to see Rocco?" Bree asks.

"I honestly have no idea," I say. "If she was, I really think she must like Rocco, for real. There's no way she'd be acting this way if he were just her friend."

"Even if he is just her friend, *we've* been her best friends for years. He's been around for—what?—a week?" Bree asks. "Why should a new friend take priority over us?"

"Right," I say. "I guess I should call her, but she probably won't even answer."

"If she does, let me know what she says," Bree tells me, lifting herself up from my bed. "So not to run, but . . ."

"You have to run," I fill in.

"Piano lessons," she says. As if on cue, a streak of light grows across the basement stairs, and Mimi's feet appear one step at a time as she descends them.

"Deirdre, dear," she says as she reaches the bottom. "Your mom is outside."

"This is Bree, Mimi," I remind her as Bree crosses the room to kiss Mimi on her cheek.

"Oh, of course," Mimi says. "How are you, dear?"

"I'm good, thanks," Bree answers as she walks back to get her things off my bed. "So sorry I have to go."

"No problem," I say. "I'll walk you out so Toby can't get a hold of you again." Bree follows me up the stairs and through the foyer, and once she is out the front door, I sit down with my back against it and close my eyes, grateful for at least a few seconds of non-accessorized quiet.

Chapter 17

When picking out my outfit the next morning, I decide that I have to be extra aware of what I wear to school from now on. After all, I'm pretty much a walking advertisement for my business, so if I want more customers, I should really look the part. I choose a fairly simple outfit so that I can let my accessories shine: jeans with a brown stitching detail running up the hems (very cowgirl-esque) with a plain white button-down shirt. I slip brown ankle-boots onto my feet, and then I walk up and down the accessory side of Blingingham Palace, deciding.

I pick up a light tan leather stretchy headband and pull it over my head and then up through my hair, pushing the strands off my face. I arrange it using the small mirror I keep propped up on top of the bookshelves, making sure there's some volume in the hair above my forehead, or else the headband would look too severe. I pull my gold spiral earrings out of their container and poke them through my holes. They look just enough like lassos to fit my theme, but not too much so that it's cheesy. I choose two large statement rings and place one on each hand. Then I weave a thin gold chain through the loops of my jeans instead of a belt. Almost perfect.

I cross to the other side of the room and slip my watch, bangle, and beaded bracelet onto my right wrist, deciding to leave my left wrist empty, just for today. Then I latch my *Tess* necklace around my neck and reach down to add my locket.

No locket.

I sift through the other off-limits pieces that I had left here before the open house to make sure the locket isn't hidden under one of them.

Still no locket.

Oh no.

No, no, no, no, no, no, no.

I run back over to Blingingham Palace and search frantically in my necklace section, hoping with all hopes that I accidentally placed it here last night. Nothing.

I dart back over to my desk and crawl underneath it, pawing at the carpet and sweeping my hands from side to side, wishing that it had fallen on the ground. Still nothing.

With shaky hands I dig my phone out of my bag and call Bree.

"Did you see anyone take my locket?" I ask as soon as she answers.

"Huh?" Bree's voice still sounds groggy with sleep.

"Yesterday, did you see anyone take my locket?" I ask again. "I had it on my desk with the other jewelry I wasn't loaning out, and it's missing."

"I don't think so," Bree says. "I didn't see anyone go near your desk, but I wasn't really paying attention."

"This is bad, Bree," I say. "Bad, bad, bad. I need to find it. Mimi gave it to me, and her grandmother gave it to her, and—"

"Okay, okay, calm down," Bree says. "Let's think about this. You know you had it when you got home from school, right?"

"Yes," I answer with certainty. "I definitely remember placing it on my desk, because I laid it down in a way so that the chain wouldn't get tangled."

"So that means it had to be someone who was there last night," Bree says. "And you know it wasn't me, so that's one suspect down."

"Would one of the sixth graders have stolen it, do you think?" I ask. "I mean, maybe without knowing the jewelry on the desk was off-limits? I don't know if I explained that part to the second group that came in."

"Maybe," Bree says. "We don't know if there were any kleptos among us."

"Thanks, real helpful," I say sarcastically.

"Sorry," Bree says. "But we really don't know if it was them, so let's decide who it definitely *wasn't*. Toby?"

"It could totally be Toby," I say. "Gosh, I really, really hope it was Toby. That would make it so much easier."

"Then ask Toby," Bree says. "Before school, and if you don't get anywhere with him, we'll come up with a new plan."

"That's what I'm afraid of," I say quietly.

"What was that?"

I sigh. "I'm afraid it *wasn't* Toby. Because if it was someone else—Kayte or Ava or one of the sixth graders or . . . Deirdre—that's so much worse."

"Come on. Deirdre wouldn't do that," Bree says. "She knows how important your stuff is to you."

"Exactly, and she was mad," I say. "She left in a huff last night, and she hasn't sent me a single text since, or called me back. Maybe she took it out of spite."

"Maybe," Bree says. "Or more likely, Kayte took it. Shady McShaderson."

"Or Ava," I suggest. "She's mad at me too. Really, how am I supposed to know who I can trust?"

"You can trust me," Bree says. "I promise, I didn't take it. Go try to shake some information out of your brother."

"Okay," I say. "Pray that he has it."

"Crossing my fingers, toes, legs, arms, and tongue now," Bree says. "Good luck." I hang up and throw my phone back into my bag before hurrying up the stairs.

"Toby!" I call as soon as I reach the top. "I need to speak to you!"

I meet Toby in his room, away from Mom's, Dad's, or Mimi's ears. None of them can know that the locket is missing, especially not Mimi. She's the one who trusted me with it, and the one who defended me to Mom. I need to try to fix this first on my own.

"Do you want to make a deal?" I ask him. Toby sits up straighter on his bed, and I can tell he's intrigued.

"What kind of deal?" he asks.

"How would you like to make five dollars?" I ask him.

"Very, very much!" Toby answers.

"So do you agree that you will do whatever I say right now, and I'll give you five dollars?" I ask. Losing five bucks from my earnings last night is the least I can do to get my locket back.

"Yes!" Toby answers. "What is it?"

"I need you to give me every single thing you've taken

from my room," I say. "Right now. This is very important. And if I get each item back—and I know exactly
what is missing—you will get your five dollars, fair and
square. Got it?"

"Got it good!" Toby says, hopping off his bed. He
darts around his room from one corner to another, collecting items that, truth be told, I did not actually know
were missing. I really have to do a better job of keeping
him out of my room unsupervised.

"Here you go." Toby places a pile into my hands:
my blue tie-dye kneesocks, my daisy-shaped sun-
glasses, my cat-face ring, a stuffed beanbag beagle
from my pile of pillows, and three button pins with
funny phrases on them.

But no locket.

"Are you absolutely positive this is everything?" I
ask, as if I know he's lying. "I'm pretty sure something
else is still missing."

Toby's eyes grow wide. "I promise," he answers, with
almost a whimper in his voice. "That is everything!"

I slump my shoulders, disappointed. It's not a great
feeling to wish for your brother to be a thief, but it was a
better alternative than what I face now.

"Okay," I say. "If you're sure . . ."

"I'm positive!" Toby tells me. "We made a deal,
remember?"

"I'll give you five dollars after school, just like I promised," I tell him. "This way, you don't have to worry about losing it all day. Okay?"

"Yes," Toby says, flying out of his room and down the stairs. "Woooo, I get five whole dollars!"

I glance around Toby's room once more before I leave, hoping to see the locket sparkling in a corner. But instead the same dreaded feeling I had earlier this morning returns—the feeling that told me deep down that Toby was never the one who took my necklace in the first place. That would have been too simple, too predictable, something eight-year-old boys just do.

Instead I now have to consider all of the other people in my life who I'm no longer sure I can trust, if I ever trusted them in the first place. Which is an even worse thing to think about than the lost locket itself, and Mimi's face when she finds out it might be gone for good.

Chapter 18

I walk in the front door of school and almost run straight into Ms. Castleby, who is leaving the main office.

"Oh good, just the person I wanted to see," Ms. Castleby says to me. "Are you still up for going on a little shopping expedition for me? For your full rate, of course."

"Yes, I'd love to!" I say, and as hard as it is, I try to push my own worries aside and concentrate on my customer, which is what a good businessperson is supposed to do. "Did you decide on what you're looking for?"

"Not exactly," Ms. Castleby says. "This is why I need you. My high school reunion is this Saturday, and I'm just looking for something to fancy up my outfit a little. I'm always drawn to the same type of stuff when I go shopping, so I could use a fresh set of eyes."

"No problem," I say, walking with Ms. Castleby down the long center hallway toward the seventh-grade wing. "Describe your outfit to me, and I'll find the perfect thing." Ms. Castleby does, and I text myself all of the information, along with important details like whether or not her ears are pierced (they are), belt size (medium), and any strong likes or dislikes (she hates the color orange—I knew there was a reason I liked her).

"Remind me of the cost again?" Ms. Castleby asks.

"Ten dollars, plus the price of the item," I say.

"And you're sure you'll have time to do this? I know I'm not giving you much notice."

"Absolutely. I can go today after school," I tell her. "I know for a fact that my brother will want to head into town anyway—the ice cream needs of eight-year-old boys and all."

Ms. Castleby laughs. "And sorry, I should've gotten it together so your payment would be in the mail already. Is it still okay if—"

"Don't worry about it. It's completely fine," I say. "You can send it to me afterward, once you make sure you like what I choose, of course. I can always return it if you don't."

"I'm sure I will, but I'll owe you the ten no matter what," Ms. Castleby says. "I'll put it in the mail for you tomorrow, just so we don't break any school policies!"

"Sounds good," I say. "Thanks for the support."

"You sound very official as a business owner," Ms. Castleby says. "I'm impressed. See you in class." She continues down the hall to her room while I twist my locker combination.

"Well, was it Toby?" Bree's voice reaches me before she does.

"No, unfortunately," I say. "So what do I do now?" I whisper this second part in case any of the potential suspects is eavesdropping on us.

"Start with Deirdre," Bree says. "You can at least ask her if she saw anyone take it."

"She'll think I'm accusing her," I say. "And she's grumpy enough as it is. If she thinks I'm calling her a thief, she may never forgive me."

"Well, what did she bring to your house yesterday? Just her book bag?"

"I don't know," I say. "I thought it was her gym bag and not her book bag, but I could be wrong."

"No, I think that's right. And she always brings that bag to lunch, since she has gym in the afternoon. So we'll look in there," Bree suggests.

"Without her knowing?"

"Yes," Bree says. "When she goes to buy her lunch, we'll look."

"If she even agrees to sit with us," I say. "She might

ditch us for Rocco, if she's still not speaking to me."

"I'll try to make sure she doesn't," Bree tells me. "Don't worry about it. I've got your back."

"Okay," I say. "But I feel weird about this."

"It's a weird situation," Bree agrees. "I mean, I'm ninety-five percent sure Deirdre wouldn't do that, but she *has* been acting strange lately, so who knows? Maybe she's changed." I follow Bree into our homeroom, and we both take our seats. Deirdre gives Bree a small smile, but she doesn't even look in my direction.

And if she won't look at me now, what is she going to do if she finds out that I think she may have stolen my locket?

Deirdre throws her gym bag down onto the bench next to me at our regular cafeteria table, but she walks away to get in line without saying one word. She has avoided me all morning, though I haven't gone out of my way to talk to her either, so I guess we're even. I keep my eyes on her until I see her join the end of the line, which thankfully seems to be moving pretty slowly today, and then I look at Bree.

"Now?" I ask.

"Now," Bree agrees.

I unzip Deirdre's bag and pull all the larger contents out onto the table in one swift motion. Deirdre's gym bag is more packed than most because she keeps a lot of her gymnastics gear in it also. I dig through the bottom of the bag as Bree rifles through the things on the table. I feel metal against my fingertips and clasp my hand around the object. I yank it from the bag and hold it out in front of me, triumphant.

Her house key.

"Ugh," I say, placing the key on the table and diving back into the bag. My hand reaches around another item, and I pull it out—Deirdre's wallet. Could she have hidden the locket in the wallet? I unsnap it and peer inside each of the slots, and then I shuffle through the coins in the change purse.

"What do you think you're doing?"

Goose bumps appear instantly on the back of my neck. I don't need to look up to know who's speaking—I'd recognize Deirdre's voice anywhere. I glance over at Bree before facing Deirdre, and Bree's face is red with guilty shock, which I assume is how mine must look too.

"You're stealing money from me?" Deirdre yells. "Is this what it's come to? How did you even know I forgot to bring my wallet up with me?"

I think about lying. I think about going with the second half of Deirdre's story, and saying that I was trying to pull money out of her wallet to bring to her in line, because I knew she had forgotten it. Would that be better or worse than the truth?

"Did you take Tess's locket?" Bree asks before I can decide. "Yesterday, at her house, did you take it off her desk?"

"I don't even know what to say to that," Deirdre replies, crossing her arms over her chest. "I can't believe you think I would take anything from either of you, ever."

"Well, you were mad when you left," I remind her. "So I just wondered . . . I didn't think you took it. I really didn't. But I wanted to make sure before I accused anyone else."

"So you accuse your best friend before you accuse, say, *Kayte Reynolds*?" Deirdre snaps.

"You haven't exactly been acting like yourself lately," I tell her quietly. "Just saying."

Deirdre glares at me—not even a glirk, but a full-on glare. "What's that supposed to mean?"

"I don't know. You're just being kind of weird," I tell her. "Like you're hiding something all the time. And look, I think Rocco is a great guy, so if you really do like him or whatever—"

"How many times do I have to tell you two? I do not like Rocco," Deirdre says matter-of-factly. "I don't understand why you keep bringing him up."

"Because ever since we found out you two were friends,

or whatever you are, you've just been . . . different," Bree explains.

Deirdre sits down on the bench and begins placing all of her things back in her gym bag. "Rocco's not just my friend," she finally tells us.

"I knew it!" Bree calls out proudly. "You like him!"

"I *don't* like him," Deirdre says. "I like him as a friend, absolutely, but I don't like him as a boyfriend."

"So then what is he?" I ask. "If he's not just your friend."

Deirdre sighs before answering. "He's my tutor," she confesses. "He's been helping me with my schoolwork. My parents made me agree to it—they said if my grades didn't improve, I was going to have to cut back on my gymnastics hours, or quit altogether. It was either that or let Rocco tutor me."

Bree and I sit in silence for a second before I respond, "That's what the big secret about Rocco was? That he's your tutor?"

"It's embarrassing!" Deirdre cries. "First of all, the fact that I need a tutor, and second of all, that someone in our own grade is doing it." She pauses. "I didn't want you to make fun of me."

"We wouldn't have made fun of you," Bree assures her.

"Oh please," Deirdre begins. "Making fun of each other is kind of our thing. And usually I love it. That's

148

what makes our friendship ours—the way we talk to one another, and can tease each other in a fun way. But I just didn't want to talk about the tutor thing. And I really didn't want other people finding out—people like Kayte Reynolds, for instance."

"So is Rocco your friend?" I ask. "Or is he just your tutor?"

"No, he's becoming my actual friend," Deirdre says. "He's a really great guy, and he completely gets why I don't want other people to know he's helping me. We actually kind of have fun together now, even when we're doing, like, our pre-algebra homework."

"So maybe you do like him," Bree persists.

"Maybe I will, someday," Deirdre answers honestly. "But not today."

"Fine," Bree says. "So no more secrets between us?"

"Um, until you two stop rifling through my belongings, looking for evidence against me, I'd say there are still some secrets," Deirdre says.

"That was my fault," I tell her. "This lost locket thing has made me crazy. I'm sorry. Really. And I'm sorry I didn't tell you that Kayte might come last night, and I'm sorry we made you feel bad about Rocco."

"Thank you," Deirdre says. "And I'm sorry I lied to you. I should have trusted you about the tutoring thing."

"I'm sorry too," Bree begins, "for everything we're

all apologizing for. I just want us to still be friends."

"We are friends, always," Deirdre says. "Okay?"

"Okay," I agree. "Now go get your lunch." I hand over her wallet. "Because I could really use a friend right now."

"About what?" Deirdre asks.

"Locket Gate," Bree says. "We need a plan of attack. And you're the best schemer of any of us, so you can figure out next steps."

"You got it," Deirdre says. "I'll be right back."

"Don't forget the ketchup!" Bree calls after her, pointing to her bagged lunch. Deirdre gives us a thumbs-up as she joins the end of the line, and I lean back against the wall of the cafeteria, suddenly exhausted.

"Do you think she's back to her old self?" I ask Bree.

"Back and better than ever," Bree says, biting into her sandwich. I can only hope that she's right, and that just like Deirdre, my locket will soon be back and better than ever too.

Chapter 19

D eirdre insists that the only way to proceed is to confront Kayte head-on about whether or not she stole the locket. I had scanned her up and down when we were in Dimmer Switch's class this morning, but since she never wears any accessories anyway, it wasn't hard to tell that she didn't have it on.

But the fact that she isn't wearing it doesn't necessarily mean that she didn't take it. In fact, it would be pretty dumb to wear something you stole. And since we don't have any surefire way to search through Kayte's book bag—or, even better, through her entire house— without her knowledge, Deirdre is on a mission. It's as if our best-friend squabble has made her resolve to take "being on my side" to a new extreme.

The minute the last bell rings at the end of the day,

the three of us head off to stand in front of Kayte's locker, and wait. She soon appears in her multi-patterned shirt that looks a bit like a quilt, paired with very tight black jeans and knee-high boots. She tosses her straight blond locks over her shoulder when she sees us, as if she knows she's preparing for battle.

"Look what the fashion police dragged in," she begins. "Decorate any sixth graders today, Maven?"

"Cut the nonsense, Reynolds," Deirdre says, a blaze in her eyes. "You know why we're here."

Kayte looks at us blankly. "Sorry, I don't have a PhD in irrationality." I raise my eyebrow and glance at Bree, who looks just as confused as I do.

"Give it back," Deirdre says. "Give it back, or we'll make sure that you do."

"I have nothing to return to the likes of you," Kayte says, trying to push past us to her locker.

"Kayte, please." I try a new tactic. "That locket is really important to me. It's a family heirloom. If you have it, just hand it over, no questions asked. Please." Kayte turns her back on Bree and Deirdre and stares only at me.

"That big honking thing you've been wearing around your neck all week?" she asks. "Yeah, guess what? The 1800s called—they want their baubles back."

"Kayte," I plead. "I'm begging you."

"I don't have your locket, Maven," Kayte says. "I mean, really. I know we're not exactly best friends anymore, but accusing me of being a thief? That's low. Even for you three."

"You're a liar, though," Deirdre pipes up again. "We established that in fifth grade, didn't we? You lie. So you're probably lying now."

"I'm not lying!" Kayte yells, with much more passion in her voice than I've heard from her since, well, fifth grade. "Maybe if you three actually listened to anyone but each other for once, you'd know that."

"You never even apologized, by the way," Deirdre continues. "For the record, you never did. After all these years, you never once said 'I'm sorry' for the lies you told about me. That's what friends do—they apologize when they do something wrong. And you wonder why we're not friends with you anymore."

"Oh please," Kayte says. "You're the one who turned these two against me, just because you wanted to." She points to Bree and me, focusing her attention on Deirdre. "You blew everything way out of proportion."

"You told everyone that I peed myself on the playground!" Deirdre shrieks, I'm sure much more loudly than she meant to.

"You *did* pee yourself!" Kayte protests. "What's the big deal?"

"It was in kindergarten!" Deirdre exclaims. "You made it seem like it had just happened. It was humiliating!"

"It could have been funny," Kayte says. "But you had to make such a big deal out of it, and then it was just—poof. You were all gone." Bree's and my eyes dart back and forth between them, as if we're watching a Ping-Pong match. I remember this big fight—the one that made Kayte (then just Kate) our enemy instead of our friend. But I never knew all of the details. Deirdre never spoke of it again, and Kayte— Well, what she did *was* wrong. She didn't need to embarrass Deirdre like that. But was it really such a huge deal? Was it a big enough problem for us all to despise one another for these past two years?

After all, we used to be the Fabulous Foursome. That's what we called ourselves all through fourth grade. It was the four of us, always.

Until it wasn't.

"Kayte." Her name is out of my mouth before I can think better of what I'm going to say. "I'm sorry." Kayte stands still in front of her locker, her hand poised and ready to twist her combination, but she keeps it there without moving. "I'm sorry," I repeat. "I'm sorry this got so out of hand." Kayte turns around then and faces us all one by one. She is quiet for so long that I'm almost afraid she is going to do something drastic. Like slap us.

154

"Thank you," she finally says, and I shoot a quick glance to Deirdre, trying to see if she is back to being mad at me again. But she looks oddly calm.

"I'm sorry too," Kayte continues, and I try not to look shocked at how easily the words come from her mouth. "I'm sorry your locket is missing." I nod my head. "I promise I didn't take it, but if you want, I'll try to help figure out who did. And I'm sorry for telling everyone you peed yourself." She says this last part just to Deirdre, but the comment makes Bree's shoulders start to shake. She squints her eyes closed, and for a moment I think she's crying.

Until a sputter of laughter escapes from her lips.

Deirdre, Kayte, and I all look at her, waiting for an explanation, but it takes Bree a few seconds to pull herself together enough to speak. "I mean, it's just so ridiculous, right?" she says. "'I'm sorry for telling everyone you peed yourself.' It sounds so silly when you say it that way." And seeing Bree laugh seems to trigger something in all of us—first me, then Deirdre, and finally even Kayte. Laughing over the same thing. Not at one another, for once, but *with* one another.

And for the first time in more than two years, it seems like we are right back where we should have been all along.

I arrive at Toby's bus stop prepared with a five-dollar bill tucked into my pocket, plus extra money to buy Ms. Castleby's accessory. As soon as he is off the bus, I hand Toby the bill with a flourish. "What do you say to buying yourself some ice cream in town?" I ask him.

"Yes!" Toby answers. "Let's go." He takes his scooter from me and wheels himself down the sidewalk in the direction of Twining Ridge Road, Mimi and me following behind.

"What was that for?" Mimi asks me.

"I promised him five dollars if he gave me back everything he took from my room," I explain. "Sort of like a bribe, which probably wasn't the best idea." I leave out the part about the missing locket—I just can't bring myself to confess that detail to Mimi yet. "When we get to town, do you want to take him for ice cream while I stop by Threads? I'm shopping for a client, but I shouldn't be too long."

"Listen to you, sounding so grown-up," Mimi says. "Yes, I'll take your brother. You take care of business." We part ways in front of Threads's window, and Mimi and Toby agree to meet me back here as soon as they are finished at the ice cream shop. I go inside, breathe in the ever-present smell of hickory, and head straight to the accessory section in the back. I begin combing through the items with my eyes, examining each one and trying to decide.

"Can I help you with anything, lovely?" the same salesgirl from last week asks.

"I don't think so," I tell her. "I'm still browsing, but thanks."

"Just let me know if you need help," she says, returning to the front counter.

"Thank you. I will," I say, and then I go back to searching. I try to picture in my head the outfit Ms. Castleby described: a blue dress, the color of a summer sky, thin straps, to the knee, fit in the waist and flared at the bottom. What will make that outfit pop instantly? A hat? Too risky. A belt? Maybe, but it would have to be the right one. A hair piece? I forgot to ask how she's planning to wear her hair. A piece of jewelry?

A bracelet won't do much, especially if she wears a cardigan with the dress. Same with a ring. But a necklace—a necklace could work. I scan through each of Threads's choices, many of which I've seen before, until I find it: a three-strand chain with tiny white sea-shells and other ocean items hanging across them. Star-fish and conch shells and sea horses, all in a row. It's beautiful. It's special without being gaudy. It will match her summer sky–blue dress perfectly.

It also looks a lot more expensive than its $14.50 price tag.

I pick the necklace up off the display table and bring it to the front. I pay for it with some of my funds from yesterday, and I'm sure to collect the receipt so I can charge Ms. Castleby the correct amount. I walk out of Threads and look down at my watch. Mimi and Toby should be back soon. I lean against the front window and pull out my phone, hoping to see a text from someone—anyone—saying they found my locket. But no such luck.

I don't want to confront Gianna or her friends about the locket. Not yet. I can't get on the bad side of customers so soon, at least not without ruling out every other suspect.

Like Ava.

Ava has to be the one who took it. She's the only other person who was on that side of my room for a significant amount of time, with no one watching her. Plus, she made such a big deal about the locket in the first place. She clearly wanted it. She was obviously jealous that Mimi had given it to me instead of to her.

She has it. The more I think about it, the more positive I become.

Quickly, before Mimi and Toby return, I tap out a text

to Ava: I know you stole my locket. Who's the spoiled brat now?

I send the text before I can think better of it, and then I place my phone back into my pocket, somehow both hoping for and dreading her reply.

Chapter 20

It turns out I had no reason to fear Ava's response, since I didn't receive one at all. To me, this only makes her seem guiltier, and by Friday morning I can barely concentrate on finding clothes that don't clash, let alone choosing a bunch of appropriate accessories. I throw on whatever catches my eye first and dart up the stairs to the kitchen, ready to scarf down breakfast before going to school and trying to finish preparing my speech for Ms. Castleby's class.

Ms. Castleby! I almost forgot her necklace. I run back down the stairs and retrieve it from my desk. I toss it, along with the receipt, into my bag. Then I return to the kitchen and pull a carton of yogurt out of the refrigerator. Toby is already at the table, slurping through a bowl of cereal, with Mimi seated beside him.

I grab a spoon and join them, sliding onto my usual chair across from Mimi.

Which is when I see it. A vision that makes me want to laugh, cry, and gasp all at the same time. Which is kind of what I end up doing.

There, right in front of me, is the locket. Safe and perfect.

Hanging around Mimi's neck.

Mimi and Toby both stare at me, waiting for me to explain the sputtering sounds coming from my mouth. "Mimi," I finally begin. "That locket."

"Oh yes." Mimi reaches up and clasps the heart in her hand, just like I did every day when it hung around my neck. "Isn't it lovely? My grandmother gave it to me when I was a little girl."

"But—but," I stammer, wishing Toby weren't at the table, hearing all of this. "You gave that locket to me. Last Saturday. You gave it to me."

Something happens in Mimi's eyes then—not the blank look of forgetfulness, but another sad gaze. It seems to be the look of recognition.

"Oh dear," Mimi says, reaching behind her head and trying to unclasp the chain. "I saw it in your room and just assumed . . ." Mimi trails off, struggling to remove the necklace.

"No, it's okay," I say. Why did I have to tell her she

161

had given it to me? It was hers, after all. She can have it back if she wants. "You keep it on. Really. I just—I thought someone had stolen it. Because I left it on my desk when all of those girls came over for the open house, and it was gone once they left. But . . ." My mind flashes back to Mimi coming down to the basement to tell Bree that her mom had arrived. Only she forgot it was Bree—she called her Deirdre. She was having a bad memory moment, so when she saw the locket, she must have thought it had been misplaced, that she was simply retrieving it, because it was hers to begin with.

"No, Tessie, it's yours," Mimi says. "Oh, I just can't . . ." She swoops the back of the chain around to the front, still working to undo the clasp.

"I'll help you, Mimi." Toby rises from his seat, and with a quick flick of his fingers, he opens the chain and tries to place the two ends of the necklace in Mimi's hands.

"Go put it on your sister," Mimi says. "Thank you, my boy."

"Are you sure?" I ask her. "Really, it's yours. We can share—"

"No, it's yours," Mimi says. "Forever. Something to remember me by." Toby closes the chain around the back of my neck as Mimi rises from the table, heading for the sink. She kisses the top of my head on her way, missing the mist of tears that have gathered in the corners of my eyes.

"Problem," I say in greeting to Deirdre and Bree as soon as I get to school.

"Your locket!" Bree exclaims. "Where was it?"

"Yeah, about that . . . ," I begin. "So I haven't really told you guys about this, but Mimi, well, she's been having some memory issues. That's why she moved in with us over the summer. She's been a little . . . off. But just sometimes. Sometimes she's completely fine, and other times, not so much."

"Sorry, friend," Deirdre says. "We kind of figured something was up, but you never seemed to want to talk about it, so we didn't push."

"Yeah, I didn't," I say. "I still don't, a lot of the time, because it makes me sad to think about. But anyway, Mimi just gave me that locket on Saturday—it was a gift her own grandmother had given her. And when she saw it on my desk on the night of the open house, she must have assumed she had left it there. Then she was wearing it this morning, so when I saw it—I mean, it was a relief, but also a problem."

"Why a problem?" Bree asks. "You have it back."

"Because in the meantime I accused all of these other

people of stealing it," I answer. "Including one of my best friends. Including my cousin."

"Egh, don't worry about me," Deirdre says. "Water under the bridge. Which cousin? Ava?"

"Yes," I confirm. "I sent her a nasty text about it last night, which she hasn't responded to yet. But she's been annoyed with me anyway, for reasons I can't even quite figure out, so this could be it between us. Accusing people of being thieves doesn't tend to go over well, as you know."

"Why don't you just try apologizing?" Bree asks. "You seem to be pretty good at doing that lately. But I would call her to do it. No more texting."

"She probably won't even take my call," I say.

"You can still try," Deirdre says. "No harm in trying."

I sigh. "Okay. I have to run this necklace over to Ms. Castleby. I got it for her to wear to her high school reunion tomorrow. I hope she likes it."

"Ooh, is that your first ten-dollar sale?" Bree asks.

"Yep," I answer proudly. "Nothing like your teacher being your best customer."

"That's because you're her favorite," Deirdre says. "Like I've always told you."

I give her one of my best glirks in response, grateful that I'm able to do so with her again.

"By the way," Deirdre says, "since we decided no

164

more secrets, I'm telling you two now that Rocco and I are going to the movies this weekend. But it's *not* a date—it's more of a thank-you to him for helping me. I'm telling you this up front so you don't accuse me of it being a date later!"

"That's so cute," I say. "Thanks for telling us."

"Just make sure he doesn't eat too much popcorn," Bree teases her, nudging Deirdre's elbow.

"Rude!" Deirdre exclaims, but she still laughs about it with us.

"So I have some news too," Bree says with a sigh. "I didn't make first chair."

Deirdre and I both move in to hug her, repeating "Aww, I'm so sorry" over and over, but Bree pushes us away.

"But I did make second chair," Bree announces. "Which means the only person better than me is Akika Watkins. Who's pretty much the best middle school flute player in the entire state, so I don't know why I ever thought I could beat her."

"Then that's awesome," Deirdre tells her. "How's Frida taking the news?"

"Very funny," Bree says, and now it's her turn to glirk.

"Plus, Akika's an eighth grader, right?" I add. "Which means next year you'll definitely be first chair."

"Yes, unless one of your little sixth-grade minions

165

comes nipping at my heels," Bree teases me. "Isn't their big dance tonight?"

"It is. Thanks for the reminder," I say. "I'll text them and tell them to have fun. Because, you know, I hear good business is all about the personal touch. I'll see you guys in homeroom."

I cross the hallway and head through Ms. Castleby's door, where I present her with the necklace I chose. Just as Deirdre and Bree predicted, she loves it, and she examines each of the shells and sea items one by one as she oohs and aahs.

"I can't tell you how perfect this is," she says. "You really have a knack for this, Tess. I already know that your business plan is going to be a great one."

"Thanks," I say. "I think it's fun. And what's the expression people say—'If you do what you love, you'll never work a day in your life'? I believe it."

Ms. Castleby laughs. "I do too," she says. "I'll get the money in the mail for you today. Thank you again."

"You're very welcome," I call, leaving the room. As I trot down the hallway toward homeroom, I feel my phone buzz. I pull it out of my pocket and look down to find the preview of a new e-mail from none other than Miscellaneous Moxie.

Thank you for your fantabulous contest entry! Unfortunately . . .

I don't need to read any further to get the message. I lost. I try not to let myself feel mopey—or lemony, as Mimi would say—about it, but disappointment seeps in anyway. Which must be clear on my face, because as soon as I enter homeroom, Deirdre and Bree run up to me.

"What's wrong?"

"She didn't like the necklace?"

"Let us see it. I'm sure it's gorgeous."

"No, no, no," I say, stopping them. "It's not that. She loved the necklace. But I entered this contest on Miscellaneous Moxie's website to design a new accessory for them, and mine wasn't chosen. I just got the e-mail."

"Sorry, friend," Bree says as they both reach around to hug me. "But buck up. You're the premiere business owner of Twining Ridge Middle School. That stupid site doesn't know what they're missing." We all take our seats as the bell rings, and despite my disappointment, I have to smile. Having two best friends who will listen to your problems is one thing, but having two who will listen and then try to cheer you up is even better. And I don't need to win an online contest to know that that alone makes me very, very lucky.

Chapter 21

I enter Dimmer Switch's classroom that day with less dread than ever before. Not because I think Dimmer's lesson on parabolas is going to be so stimulating, but because for once, I may not have to spend the whole period being glared at by my seat partner. I mean, Kayte and I are on good terms again, right? Did yesterday's conversation cement that, or was that just in my head? What if things are just as hostile between us as ever before?

"You found it," Kayte says in greeting, but her face shows no emotion, so I'm not sure if this is a friendly statement or not.

"What's that?" I ask as I take my seat.

She points toward my chest. "Your locket," she clarifies. "You found it."

"Oh, yes," I say. "It's kind of a long story. Turns out it never actually left my house in the first place. I'm sorry again for accusing you."

"So where—" Kayte begins, but she stops herself, looking over my head toward the classroom door. I turn and see Ms. Castleby crossing the room toward Mr. Dimmer, and she whispers something into his ear. He nods, and Ms. Castleby looks in Kayte's and my direction, gesturing for us to follow her.

Both of us point to our chests and ask, "Me?" and for a moment, I have a flicker of a memory of when Kayte and I used to accidentally speak in unison frequently, like good friends often do. That all ended after that infamous fifth-grade fight, when I settled squarely on Deirdre's side, whether or not it was a fair choice.

"Tess and Kayte, both of you," Ms. Castleby says. "Can you come with me?"

Some of our classmates let out an "Ooooh," and Kayte and I glance at each other with questions in our eyes. We follow Ms. Castleby out of Dimmer's classroom and down the hall to her own. She doesn't say a word until we are behind her closed door, which is when she finally turns to face us.

That's when I become convinced that we really must be in trouble. Did she take a closer look at our journals? Does she now believe that we actually copied each other, or that, even worse, I copied Kayte? How can we prove that it was just a coincidence?

"I have some good news for you two," Ms. Castleby announces, and I exhale loudly, so relieved by the word "good" that I almost don't care what she says next.

Almost.

"Remember that I mentioned how closely your journal entries seemed to mimic Miscellaneous Moxie's blogging style?" she asks. "Well, I took the liberty of photograph- ing some of your pages and e-mailing them to the site, suggesting that you two be sort of 'young roving fashion commentators' for their TheBlingZone entries. Anyway, I just got an e-mail back from them, and guess what?"

She pauses, waiting for us to respond, but we both seem too stunned to say anything. At least that's how I feel.

"They loved the idea," Ms. Castleby continues. "They especially loved the fact that you two tend to agree on, well, very little when it comes to your fashion opinions. I sent them your entries on glitter, for instance, where, Tess, you talk about how great faux glitter accessories are, and, Kayte, you hate fake glitter products. Any- way, this really got their attention, and they said in their e-mail that they'd like to try to make you two like a 'yin and yang' pairing, proving how subjective fashion tastes and choices are.

"I know this is a lot to digest at once," she continues. "But if you're interested—"

"We're interested!" I blurt out. "I mean, I'm interested. Kayte, are you interested?"

"I'm definitely interested," she answers. "Not just interested—we should absolutely do it."

"I agree," I say. "Ms. Castleby, thank you! This is amazing!"

"Of course," she answers. "I think it will be a great opportunity for both of you. If it's okay with you, I'll e-mail your parents this weekend and get their permission first, and if they approve, I'll get back to Miscellaneous Moxie and tell them that you're in."

"Perfect," Kayte says. "Is there anything we should do in the meantime?"

"You could brainstorm some ideas for your columns—especially things going on in the fashion world that you might have opposite opinions on," she says. "And I think each of you should come up with a pen name. For security reasons, they probably won't want seventh graders using their real names on the site. So think about what you'd like to go by."

"Sounds great," I say. "I'm so excited!"

"I am too," Kayte agrees. "This is awesome."

"Oh, and I might as well give these back to you now," Ms. Castleby says, walking over to her desk and retrieving our journals. "Needless to say, you each got an A+. I really enjoyed reading them."

We thank Ms. Castleby again and practically skip out the door. "Good thing we had that chat yesterday, huh?" I ask Kayte. "Or else this could be really awkward right now."

The comment actually makes Kayte laugh hard—the first time I have made her laugh this heartily in more than two years, and I'm surprised to realize how much I like hearing it again. "You're right," she says. "I assume you're going to go by 'Bling Queen' on the site?"

"Wow, I didn't even think that far ahead yet," I say. "But yeah, I think that's a good idea. What about you?" I think back to what Kayte called herself on that ExtraUniverse post. "'Glitz Girl'?"

"Do you like that?" Kayte asks. "Or is it cheesy?"

"No, I think it's great," I say. "Glitz Girl and Bling Queen."

"Middle school's most opinionated fashionistas," Kayte adds, which then makes me laugh. We are just approaching Dimmer's door when Mrs. Latara appears at the other end of the hallway.

"Hey, excuse me!" she calls. "Weren't you the girl looking for a ring before?"

"Yes!" I call down the corridor. "Yes, I was."

"Someone turned one in," Mrs. Latara continues.

"Earlier today I noticed one in a corner of a bin. Lucky I saw you here. You know I don't normally police the Lost and Found."

"Wow, really? Do you think it's mine?" I ask. "Can I go to your office and check?"

"Be my guest," Mrs. Latara says. "The door should be open."

"Do you mind telling Mr. Dimmer that I'll be back in a few minutes?" I ask Kayte. "Make sure he doesn't lock me out and all?"

"Sure," she says. "I hope you find what you're looking for." She gives me a small smile as she reaches for the doorknob.

"Me too," I call over my shoulder, hurrying to the Lost and Found. "Thank you, Mrs. Latara!" I walk briskly through the hallways all the way to the front of the school, trying my best not to run. I dart into the nurse's office and over to the Lost and Found, and I rifle through the bins one by one. And there in the corner, all the way to the left, is my infinity ring. Looking a little less sparkly than it did last week, but there all the same. I pick it up carefully and slip it onto my ring finger, where it will be tighter than on my pinkie. Then I run my other hand's index finger over the infinity symbol again and again, which gives me a great idea for Glitz Girl and Bling Queen's first entry:

I pull my phone out of my pocket and text Kayte, **What do you think about infinity rings becoming the new friendship bracelets? Like friends exchange them with each other, symbolizing that their friendships will go on forever?**

I walk back to Dimmer's classroom and take my seat, while everyone pretends to listen to him drone on about the *y* parabola axis. I rip a sheet out of my notebook and write, *Did you get my text?* and then slip the paper onto Kayte's desk.

Yes. Friendship bracelets are so corny. Infinity friendship rings even cornier = we have our first entry! she writes back.

I draw a smiley face on the paper before crinkling it and placing it on the corner of my desk. It seems the yin and yang of fashion advice are off to a blazing start.

Chapter 22

Once we return that afternoon from picking Toby up at his bus stop, I head to my room and send fast texts to all of the sixth graders who borrowed accessories from me for the dance. **Hi, Ellie! I hope you and the suspenders have a bling-worthy time at the dance tonight!** I personalize every text with the girl's name and what they chose from Blingingham Palace, since I think the key to good business is making each customer feel special. Once that task is finished, I sit up straight on my couch and take a deep breath, dreading the call that comes next.

I press Ava's name on my phone before I can procrastinate doing so any longer, and I instantly regret it. She probably won't answer me, and then what? Should I just hang up and wait for her to see my missed call?

Should I try again later? Should I leave a voice message? But what would I say? I really should have planned this out better before placing the call.

"Hello?" Ava answers after the third ring. No turning back now.

"Hi," I begin. "It's Tess."

"I see that." Cold.

Uh-oh.

"Look, I'm calling to say I'm sorry." I decide to launch directly into my apology, like pulling off a bandage in one swift motion rather than dragging out the process. "I was really upset about the locket being missing, but I shouldn't have accused you of taking it. And I definitely shouldn't have sent you that text. I'm sorry."

Ava doesn't respond at first, and for a moment I'm afraid she's not going to at all. Just before I am about to apologize again, she finally asks, "Did you find it?"

"The locket?"

"Of course the locket."

"Yes," I answer. "It turns out Mimi took it off my desk by accident. I think she forgot that she had given it to me. So when she saw it there, she must have assumed she had misplaced it."

"Wow," Ava says. "So you found it in her room?"

"No, she was wearing it at breakfast this morning," I explain. "I don't think I handled it very well, actually.

Maybe I shouldn't have said anything about it at all. But I was just so shocked to see it that I couldn't help myself."

"What happened? What did you say?" Ava asks. She still doesn't exactly sound friendly, but at least she's speaking to me.

"I reminded her that she had given the locket to me," I say. "But I think I embarrassed her, because I'm not sure how much Mimi realizes she doesn't remember, you know? I just felt bad, but once it was out of my mouth, I couldn't take it back."

"I wouldn't feel too bad," Ava tells me. "The memory stuff is hard to deal with, and you have to do it all the time."

"It's really not so bad," I say. "She's just regular Mimi most of the time. Then there are . . . episodes. She called Toby by Uncle Carl's name a couple of days ago. She doesn't usually do that."

Ava becomes quiet, and for a second I think she must have hung up. "Are you there?" I ask.

"Yeah, sorry," Ava says. "That happened to me the last time Mimi was over. Not this past weekend but the time before. She forgot my name."

"She doesn't mean to," I say. "I don't even think she realizes she does it at the time."

"She called me 'Tess.'" Ava waits a beat. "Like, she

thought I was you. And she said something about how much she loved you and all that."

I listen, reading between the lines of what Ava is saying. If Mimi told me to my face that I'm her favorite grandchild, maybe she told Ava this as well—only because she thought she was talking to me. I know Mimi would never purposely hurt Ava's feelings. And I also know that she loves Ava to pieces, just like she loves all of her grandchildren.

"She's told me that you're her favorite before," I blurt out to Ava.

"Really?" Ava asks.

"Yes," I say. "Sometimes you're her favorite grand-child, sometimes Hayden or Harper, or Anderson or Toby. We all seem to rotate." I figure I'm not exactly lying to Ava. Mimi has always said that she loves each of her grandchildren in his or her own unique way. And plus, I think this will make Ava feel better. No one likes to feel forgotten, whether Mimi means to or not.

"Wow," Ava says. "I'm really sorry, then. I took it out on you for no reason. I never knew she said those things. It just seemed like . . . like she still remembered every-thing about you, and nothing about me."

"So you got jealous," I say. "We all get jealous some-times."

"That's true," Ava says. "So can we go back to being

normal again? I really don't like fighting with you, even though I know I'm the one who started it. Plus, I need to make sure I have my maid of honor lined up for my hypothetical wedding."

I laugh at Ava. Someday, we *will* be each other's maids of honor in our respective weddings, just like Harper will be at Hayden's tomorrow. After all, we're just as good as sisters. We love each other like sisters, and clearly, we can fight like sisters too.

"Of course," I say. "Let's forget the whole thing ever happened. I saw Mimi's finished scarf, by the way. You really outdid yourself."

"Thanks," Ava says. "And you're going to have to tell me more about this business you started. It seemed crazy-busy there on Wednesday. Super impressive."

"I'll tell you all about it tomorrow," I promise. "I actually presented my pitch to my language arts class today, and it went really, really well. I think I might have scrounged up a few more customers from it."

"That's awesome," Ava says. "I can't wait to hear about it."

"And I'm just glad I won't have to avoid you during the whole wedding now," I tell her.

"Me too," Ava says. "See you bright and early at the church." We hang up, and I swear I can feel a gallon of weight lift off my shoulders. I walk over to the dress section of my closet and push through each hanger. I decide that I can save the blue dress for the next big event. Tomorrow I'll wear something a different color from Ava's so that we can both stand out, each in our own unique way.

Chapter 23

The next morning I slip into a dress Mom purchased for me at Threads last year. It's magenta with silky tissue-paper-like pieces curling around like the thinnest of ruffles from top to bottom. I pair the dress with gold, shiny flats, and then I turn to my accessories. I place my infinity ring on my right hand and a ring with a large pink gemstone on my left middle finger. I put my watch, beads, and *Sparkle is my favorite color* bangle on their usual wrist, and then I choose a gold cuff with weaved detail for the left. I poke a pair of infinity drop earrings through my holes. They're small, but they dangle just enough to make me happy, with the infinity symbols hanging vertically, so that from a distance they almost look like the number eight.

I leave my hair down and free of decorations, and

even though my dress comes all the way up to my neck, I clasp on my locket and *Tess* necklace, and then tuck them both beneath the collar. Even if no one can see them, I like knowing that they're there.

I walk up two flights of stairs and pass Toby's room, where Dad is trying to wrangle him into a suit. I knock on Mimi's bedroom door, which is partially open. "Mimi?" I call.

"Come in, dear," Mimi says. "Maybe you can help me arrange this scarf." I enter and see Mimi all decked out in a pale pink dress with the silky soft jacket from Aunt Rebecca, which is simple enough that she is able to accessorize it to the max. Long sparkly earrings shimmer from either side of her head, swaying back and forth each time she moves, and she has put on her fanciest pair of beige chunky heels. As always, her hair and makeup look just as perfect as her ensemble.

Mimi, I think, is beautiful.

"You look stunning," I tell her honestly, maneuvering Ava's scarf around her neck so that it falls just right on one of her shoulders. It is the perfect completion to her look.

"Oh, you're sweet, Tessie," Mimi says. "Stand back now. Let me have a look at you. Give me a twirl." I back up and spin around so that Mimi can see the dress in action. "Just the prettiest girl in the world." Mimi takes one more glance at herself in her vanity's mirror, and then she sticks a tube of pink lipstick into a matching pink handbag.

"Oh, I almost forgot a bag!" I exclaim. "I'll meet you downstairs." I run back to my room and choose a small clutch from my handbag shelf. It catches the light in all the right ways, and it instantly makes me feel more glamorous.

Plus, while it looks glittery from a distance, it's actually made of teeny tiny rhinestones. So not only do I love it, but it also proves my point about the benefits of faux glitter items. A win on both counts!

I do one last check of myself in my full-length mirror, smoothing out the gloss on my top lip. Then I go back upstairs to the kitchen.

"Well, don't you look lovely?" Mom greets me. "But what happened to that new blue dress we got for today?"

"I decided to go with something different," I explain. "Plus, I can wear that to Harper's wedding. I'm sure she won't let Hayden be the only one married for long."

"You're probably right," Mom says. "So I received an e-mail this morning from Ms. Castleby. One about you writing your own fashion column?"

"Oh . . . yes," I say. "But I promise it won't take away from my schoolwork, and I promise I'll keep my grades up and do responsible things and be conscientious." I talk quickly, hoping the sound of my voice will delay Mom's announcing that I'm not allowed to do the Miscellaneous Moxie blog. "Please, if you just let me do a few entries, I'll show you that it won't change—"

"I think it's fantastic," Mom says. "It's an amazing opportunity for you. We already knew that no one loves accessories like you do, but Ms. Castleby says that based on the journal you did for her class, you really know how to write about them too. I'm proud of you, Tess."

"Really?" I say. "I mean, thank you."

"And don't think I haven't noticed how great you've been with Mimi these past few months. I know it wasn't easy having her move in with us, and you've really stepped up to the plate, caring for her."

"I love Mimi," I say. "You know that."

"Of course you do," Mom says. "But that still doesn't mean this hasn't been an adjustment, for all of us. I mean, you even have a new room."

"And it's the best room ever," I say. "Really, I'm glad Mimi moved in. Because I like seeing her every day, but I also love my new space. I named it Blingingham Palace."

"Well, that sounds perfect," Mom says. "So in case you were wondering, that jewelry exhibition at the museum in a couple of weeks? We'll go. After that A+ you received on your language arts journal, you definitely deserve a little reward, and I figure it will be good business research for you anyway."

"Thank you!" I say. "I can't wait. I promise you'll love the show too."

"If you love it, that's good enough for me," Mom says, smiling. "Now let's get going before we're late." Mom places her arm across my shoulders and leads me outside. We pile into the car, Toby squirming in the middle seat between Mimi and me, pulling at the dinosaur tie that Dad has knotted around his neck. I look around at each of them and grin. If nothing else, we are definitely one another's best accessories.

Dad pulls into a parking space directly next to Ava's family. Ava and I are so eager to get out of the car that we both almost open our doors directly into each other's.

And then the minute that we're outside, we burst out laughing.

"What are you wearing?"

"What is *that* dress?"

"I thought you were wearing blue."

"I thought *you* were wearing blue."

Ava stands in front of me in her very own magenta dress. Hers is different from mine, with a thick belt circling her waist and a large poof at her shoulders, but it is the exact same color.

Just like the cornflower-blue dresses we were supposed to be wearing were also the *exact* same color.

"I decided to wear something else," Ava tells me. "You know, since that dress was part of the reason behind our only fight ever, I thought it had bad energy."

"Oh my goodness, me too," I tell her. "Plus, I knew you really liked yours, so I figured we could each wear our own color. But this is even better."

"Absolutely," Ava agrees.

"Well, look at the two twins," Aunt Rebecca says when she sees us together. "And here I thought Hayden and Harper were going to be the only twins around today."

"Come on, Toby." Anderson places his hand on the top of Toby's buzzed hair, leading him away from us. "What do you say we find our own seats in the church, away from these weirdos?"

"Yeah!" Toby calls, running beside Anderson happily. Our parents and Mimi follow them, with Ava and me trailing behind.

"Your scarf is gorgeous, by the way," I tell Ava. "It really looks amazing on Mimi."

"Thank you," she says. "I hope she likes it."

"She loves it," I assure her. "Now, I have a very important question for you. Do you think there's any chance at all that Hayden and Harper are going to switch places today? I mean, how would any of us know if it were actually Harper getting married?"

"That is an excellent point," Ava says. "Haven't they always said that the only thing distinguishing them is a freckle that Hayden has above her belly button or something?"

"Can you imagine—that sounds like a movie, right? The bride and maid of honor switch places the day of the wedding?"

"I really wouldn't put it past them," Ava says. "Those two are crazy. Must be a twin thing."

"Agreed," I say. "Promise me that when you're my maid of honor, you won't try to marry the groom."

"I promise," Ava laughs. "And you do the same."

"You got it," I say as we walk through the front doors of the church, the sounds of a hundred bells chiming all around us. And as we do, I begin to fantasize about my own wedding day: my bridal party, my dress, the flowers. . . . And even though it's still many years—and the ability to find a husband—away, imagining it still makes me very excited.

After all, if a wedding calls for one thing, it's a whole lot of bling.

Back in the car after the ceremony, I take my phone out of my clutch and turn it on. Mom and Mimi are discussing how lovely everything was, how beautiful Hayden and Harper looked (though, if you ask me, I still can't be completely sure that it was Hayden in the wedding gown), while Toby finally manages to break free from his tie, lassoing it around his head in triumph.

I block them all out as my phone comes back to life, dinging with what seems like a thousand text messages.

Thank you so much for your help—the dance was great! Couldn't have done it without you!

I am obsessed with these suspenders, and I think they brought me luck last night. (I'll tell you about that later!) I have a bat mitzvah to go to next weekend. Do you think I could make another appointment with you?

Hi, I got your number from Gianna. I'd love to have you help me choose some new accessories for our family trip to New York in a couple of weeks. Would that be possible?

Best dance ever—thanks to you. I felt like a star! Talk again soon, Bling Queen!

Each of these messages makes me smile proudly, grateful that I was able to help these girls feel a bit more special on their big night out. I keep scrolling through my screen and find two more texts. The first is Deirdre on our group exchange with Bree, asking how the wedding is going. And the second text is from none other than Kayte Reynolds.

I quickly tap out a reply to Deirdre and Bree: **Wedding is great. I'll send you pictures from the reception. By the way, I'm putting in my request now for you two to be my bridesmaids. Clear your schedules!**

Done! And ditto! Deirdre's reply comes almost immediately, followed soon after by a **Triple ditto, whackadoos!** from Bree.

I then open Kayte's text and read. **So don't take this the wrong way, but how about as another idea, we do a piece on lockets? You obviously love them, and I—well, I don't. But I think that could set up a good debate, right?**

I love it! I type back. **Here's our title: "Lockets—Vintage Must-Haves or Stash Them with the Moth Balls?"**

Yes! Kayte replies. **This is fun. I'm glad we're on friendly terms again. Much less awkward.**

Totally, I reply. **And not just friendly—friends.**

Right, Kayte types back. **Just don't think of giving me one of those dumb infinity friendship rings of yours.**

I laugh out loud at this, and Mimi turns and looks at me. "What's so funny, Tessie?" she asks.

"Oh, nothing much," I say. "I'm just talking to my future bridesmaids."

"You're getting a little ahead of yourself, don't you think?" Mom asks.

"It's never too early to make your forever friends, right?" I ask. "Plus, I already know what I'll give them as their bridal party gift." I pause for dramatic effect. "Nameplate earrings. Just like nameplate necklaces, only they dangle down to your shoulders. I'm sure by the time I get married, I'll finally be able to get them designed."

"Sounds like a plan," Mom says, turning back around to help give Dad directions. Toby is tying the laces on his shiny black shoes into knots, and I look over his head at Mimi, catching her eye.

"By the way," I begin, retrieving the locket from underneath my dress, "you and I should try to get a picture tonight. So that I can place it in here."

Mimi's pink-painted lips spread into a huge grin. "Consider it done," she says, and we both turn away and look out our respective windows. But I keep the heart of the locket clutched in my fist. Because maybe that's really the best part of bling—who it came from, who it reminds you of, what it means to you.

I hold the locket tightly for another second, willing myself to never forget this moment. And that just might be the point, I think, of the accessories you love. They may not hug you hello and kiss you good-bye, fill you with giggles, or brush away your tears.

But they always help you remember.

Acknowledgments

Endless thank-yous to Alyson Heller for trusting me with your blingtastic idea. You are the sparkliest editor of all!

Glittery thanks to Charlie Olsen for being the snazziest agent I could ask for.

And the glitziest of appreciation to Mara Anastas, Fiona Simpson, Faye Bi, Kayley Hoffman, Jessica Handelman, Carolyn Swerdloff, and the rest of the Aladdin team for always keeping the literary baubles polished!

Check out these great titles from Aladdin M!X:

ALADDINMIX.COM

Aladdin M!X
Collect them all!

- ❏ **Saturday Cooking Club #1: Kitchen Chaos**
  by Deborah A. Levine and JillEllyn Riley

- ❏ **25 Roses** by Stephanie Faris

- ❏ **At Your Service** by Jen Malone

- ❏ **The (Almost) Perfect Guide to Imperfect Boys** by Barbara Dee

- ❏ **The XYZs of Being Wicked** by Lara Chapman

- ❏ **Lost in London** by Cindy Callaghan

- ❏ **Lost in Paris** by Cindy Callaghan

- ❏ **Best Friends (Until Someone Better Comes Along)** by Erin Downing

- ❏ **Plastic Polly** by Jenny Lundquist

- ❏ **Fake Me a Match** by Lauren Barnholdt

- ❏ **Seeing Cinderella** by Jenny Lundquist

- ❏ **Triple Trouble** by Julia DeVillers and Jennifer Roy

- ❏ **Stealing Popular** by Trudi Trueit

- ❏ **D Is for Drama** by Jo Whittemore

- ❏ **Rules for Secret Keeping** by Lauren Barnholdt

- ❏ **BFF Breakup** by Taylor Morris

DOWNLOAD A COMPLETE M!X CHECKLIST AT ALADDINMIX.COM.

EBOOK EDITIONS ALSO AVAILABLE

m!x | FROM ALADDIN | KIDS.SIMONANDSCHUSTER.COM